DROWN[...]

With his head underwater, he couldn't hear the soggy clicks the revolver was making, but he knew the weapon wasn't firing. He released it and let it sink in the fountain, then reached behind his head and tried to claw at Hector's face.

Longarm's chest felt as if it was about to explode. A red mist swam before his eyes. He knew he couldn't last much longer. . . .

DON'T MISS THESE
ALL-ACTION WESTERN SERIES
FROM THE BERKLEY PUBLISHING GROUP

THE GUNSMITH by J. R. Roberts
> Clint Adams was a legend among lawmen, outlaws, and ladies. They called him . . . the Gunsmith.

LONGARM by Tabor Evans
> The popular long-running series about U.S. Deputy Marshal Long—his life, his loves, his fight for justice.

LONE STAR by Wesley Ellis
> The blazing adventures of Jessica Starbuck and the martial arts master, Ki. Over eight million copies in print.

SLOCUM by Jake Logan
> Today's longest-running action Western. John Slocum rides a deadly trail of hot blood and cold steel.

TABOR EVANS

LONGARM

AND THE
MAN-EATERS

JOVE BOOKS, NEW YORK

LONGARM AND THE MAN-EATERS

A Jove Book / published by arrangement with
the author

PRINTING HISTORY
Jove edition / December 1994

ISBN: 0-515-11505-3

A JOVE BOOK®
Jove Books are published by The Berkley Publishing Group,
200 Madison Avenue, New York, New York 10016.
JOVE and the "J" design are trademarks
belonging to Jove Publications, Inc.

PRINTED IN THE UNITED STATES OF AMERICA

10 9 8 7 6 5 4 3 2 1

LONGARM

AND THE
MAN-EATERS

Chapter 1

The man panted from terror and exhaustion as he raced along the brush-dotted shore. Every few seconds he threw frantic glances over his shoulder, and the growing horror as his shadowy pursuers steadily closed the gap made him run even harder. His strength was ebbing away, though. It was inevitable that they would catch him.

And he knew what would happen then.

The thick saw grass along the shoreline seemed to clutch at his ankles like hands holding him back. To his right, the waters of St. Charles Bay lapped gently at a narrow beach. The half-moon floating high above in the Texas sky reflected off the water and sent silvery light washing over the landscape. It should have been a peaceful, placid scene—instead of one of impending violence and gruesome death.

The fleeing man let out a yelp of pain as he tripped suddenly over an exposed root of a scrubby, wind-twisted tree. He fell sprawling into the grass, rolling over a couple of times before he could regain his balance and leap to his feet again. His left ankle had been twisted by the accident, and tried to collapse underneath him as it felt like broken glass was being ground into the joint of the bone. He ignored the agony and began running again, prodded by the fact that his pursuers had gained even more on him. They were less than fifty yards behind him now.

Desperately, his eyes scanned the night as he ran, looking for a light or any sign of possible help. There was nothing but darkness around him. Far out in the gulf, he saw a pinprick of light that might have been a lantern on a passing ship, but it was much too far away to do him any good. His breath hissed harshly between his teeth as he held in the screams that tried to well up his throat.

The bay curved inland ahead of him. He followed the shore, resisting the impulse to turn and run away from the water. He was a seagoing man and always had been. The vast prairies of the Texas coastal plain held nothing for him. The sea, in fact, might be his salvation, he realized. If he could get far enough ahead of the killers chasing him so that they would lose sight of him momentarily, he could slip into the bay and swim underwater away from the shore. The pursuit might pass by him then without ever noticing him. He would sooner take his chances with the sharks and stingrays and jellyfish that inhabited these waters than the men behind him.

He never got the chance. A thrown club whipped through the air and crashed into the back of his head, sending him sprawling to the ground again. The blow did not knock him out, but it stunned him so that his muscles would not respond to the feverish commands sent out by his brain. All he could do was writhe on the ground and whimper as the other men caught up to him and surrounded him. They seemed gigantic as they loomed over him, blotting out the stars in the night sky overhead.

One of them reached for him. He kicked out, knowing he could not hope to escape now but determined not to die without a fight. He had cleaned out waterfront bars from Singapore to Cairo, and by God, he wasn't going to lie down like a dog now! His foot thudded against the bare chest of the man reaching for him, knocking the man back.

He rolled over and tried to get to his feet, but as he made it to his hands and knees, another club crashed down on his back and a kick slammed into his side. He collapsed again. Clubs began to rise and fall, and with each descent of the weapons, there was a chorus of ugly wet thudding sounds.

Mercifully, the man who had tried to flee stopped feeling anything after the third or fourth blow.

When the killers were done, they rolled the dead man over onto his back, and a knife blade gleamed in the moonlight as it hovered over his chest for a second, then struck. The grisly task was carried out quickly and expertly. The dead man's chest was laid open and a hand was plunged into the hollow carved by the knife. Fingers closed around a still-quivering lump of muscle and ripped it free. Blood still hot with life dripped down the arm of the man who held the heart high and proud in the moonlight.

The ritual was almost complete. Almost . . .

Chapter 2

Two things struck Longarm in the face as he stepped down off the stagecoach in Rockport, Texas. One was the wet heat of summer along the coast of the Gulf of Mexico. The other was the clenched fist of just about the biggest Mexican Longarm had ever seen.

The blow made him rock back against the coach and drop the bag he had brought with him on his trip from Denver. The big Mexican had already lunged on past with a curse after knocking Longarm out of the way. The man was chasing a gal in a white blouse and colorful skirt. Longarm had caught just a glimpse of her frightened face as she dashed by the coach while he was stepping out. She was running so hard down the street that her long, raven-dark hair was streaming out behind her. But her pursuer's long strides were steadily drawing him closer to her.

Longarm rubbed his jaw where the Mexican had so casually swatted him, then looked around. He saw cowboys from the ranches inland slouching on the porch of the saloon across from the stage station, and the sidewalks along both sides of the street were crowded with businessmen, ladies doing their shopping, sailors and stevedores from the wharves a few blocks away along the harbor, and Mexican farmers.

And not a damned one of them, as far as Longarm could see, was going to do a damned thing to help that poor gal being chased.

His jaw tightened and he reached across his body to lift the Colt .44-40 from the cross-draw rig on his left side. The temptation was to put a bullet in that big son of a bitch's back, but Longarm was, after all, an official, badge-toting deputy United States marshal and sworn to uphold the law, not to go gunning down everybody rude enough to clout him in the chops for no good reason. So he put a round between the big Mexican's sandal-clad feet instead.

The sound of the shot and the bullet kicking up dust between his feet threw the man off stride and made him lose his balance. He went tumbling head over heels just as he was about to reach out and snag the back of the girl's blouse. Longarm trotted after the Mexican as the fleeing girl darted out of sight around a corner.

It was too blasted hot for a fandango like this, Longarm thought as he stopped about ten feet from the fallen Mexican and leveled his gun at the big man. Longarm had taken off his brown tweed coat and stored it in his bag, but he still wore the matching vest and trousers and the white shirt that was stained dark with sweat. The broad brim of the flat-crowned, snuff-brown Stetson on Longarm's head shaded his already deeply tanned features from the sun. He kept the Mexican covered and ordered, "Get up slow and easy, old son, and I won't have to shoot you."

Folks all along the street had come to a halt and were watching the little drama play itself out. Longarm didn't cotton much to people staring at him, but there wasn't anything he could do about it now. Nobody had forced him to take cards in this hand. He wondered if anybody had gone running for the local law yet.

The big Mexican climbed somewhat unsteadily to his feet and glared at Longarm. He was a good six and a half feet tall, Longarm judged, with wide shoulders and arms like the trunks of small trees. His dirty white shirt had had the sleeves ripped off sometime in the past, and the white trousers he wore reached only a little below his knees. His long hair hung in filthy clumps around his head, and his beard was thick and matted enough to have varmints nesting in it. He looked furious enough to pluck the legs off an insect—or a fool lawman.

"Well, you ain't the most handsome specimen I ever saw," Longarm said. "If you had romance on your mind, mister, I can see why that gal took off a-running."

Suddenly, a voice behind Longarm spat, *"Perro!"*

Without looking back, Longarm said, "You'd best be calling your dog, friend, and not referring to me. I'm about to get the idea that visitors here ain't too welcome."

"Put your gun away, gringo, and stop threatening my servant," the imperious voice commanded.

Longarm still didn't look around. He hadn't heard the sound of a gun being cocked, and he could tell from the second gent's voice that the man wasn't close enough to stick him with a knife. Of course, he *was* within throwing distance.

With a quick step to the side, Longarm swung around so that he could swing his gun easily toward either man. The second one was much smaller than the first, not much bigger than a good-sized kid, in fact. This hombre wore a neat brown suit, a black hat, and a string tie. Town shoes that held a high polish despite the ever-present dust were on his small feet. His face was narrow and divided by a hawk nose and a narrow black mustache. His dark eyes gleamed with anger as he stared at Longarm.

"You're the one who sicced this bruiser on that gal?" Longarm asked.

"She too is my servant," the small, dapper man replied, crossing his arms and regarding Longarm arrogantly.

"He lies! El Pollo lies!"

The cry came from down the street, and Longarm glanced that way long enough to see the girl who had been running away a few minutes earlier. She was peeking hesitantly around the corner where she had disappeared, but despite her obvious

6

fright, she was still angry enough to speak up.

"El Pollo," Longarm mused as he looked back at the small man. "The Chicken. That'd be you, I reckon."

The man drew himself up, trying to look taller and more dignified. "I am Hortensio Ortiz. Some call me El Pollo."

"He is a *brujo*!" the girl yelled. "He wants to make me his slave! Do not let him, I beg you!"

"Take it easy," Longarm told her as he continued to watch both Hortensio Ortiz and the giant who evidently worked for Ortiz. "It's been a long time since old Abe Lincoln said slavery wasn't legal no more, at least on this side of the Rio Grande. There was a war fought over it, if I remember right. So you don't have to worry about anybody turning you into a slave, ma'am, even if he does claim to be some sort of witch-man."

"El Pollo does not care about gringo law," growled the big man, speaking up for the first time since knocking Longarm aside earlier. "El Pollo makes his own law!"

"Not in these parts," Longarm said firmly. "Speaking of which, where *is* the local badge-toter?"

Nobody in the watching crowd spoke up, but a few of them moved forward, and Longarm saw that all the men closing in on him were hard-faced Mexicans of the same stripe as the big gent who had started this ruckus, only smaller. They still looked plenty formidable, though, and from the smug expression on the face of Hortensio Ortiz, Longarm guessed these men were either servants or followers of the *brujo*.

All he'd gone and done was try to be a little chivalrous, and here he was in trouble again.

"Call off your dogs, Ortiz," Longarm said, letting the barrel of his revolver drift more in the direction of the smaller man. "I'm a deputy U.S. marshal, and you don't want to be doing this."

El Pollo laughed. "I do not fear you, gringo. I command the spirits of the dead, and as Hector told you, I care nothing for your law." He uncrossed his arms and barked, "Hector!" A spate of Mexican too fast for Longarm to comprehend followed, and the giant called Hector lunged at him.

For an instant, Longarm thought about shooting Ortiz anyway, but then he pivoted smoothly and let Hector's bull-like charge carry him past. Longarm reversed his grip on the Colt and chopped at the back of the big man's neck with the butt of the gun. The blow struck home but didn't seem to faze Hector, who caught his balance and swung lumberingly around as a couple of men from the crowd got into the act by jumping Longarm.

One of them grabbed the wrist of his gun hand and shoved it down, while the other wrapped his arms around Longarm and pinned the deputy marshal's arms. Both of them were dressed like farmers and wore sandals on their feet, so Longarm brought the heel of his right boot down sharply on the instep of the gent who was bear-hugging him from behind. The man yelped and loosened his grip enough for Longarm to drive an elbow back into his belly. Breath heavily laden with the smell of peppers gusted from the man's mouth.

Longarm saw Hector swinging a massive fist toward his head, so he took advantage of the second man hanging on to his wrist and jerked the man between him and Hector, who was unable to stop his fist from crashing into the back of the man's head. Longarm saw the man's eyes roll up as he sagged loosely toward the ground, and Hector let out a grunt of pain—or maybe just annoyance—at having smashed his knuckles against a hard skull. Longarm shoved the stunned hombre toward Hector, hoping he'd get in the big man's way.

The other Mexican was still grappling with Longarm from behind. Longarm stomped his foot again, then twisted at the waist and swung the gun butt toward the man's head. The man tried to jerk back, but the gun still caught him a glancing blow and made him stumble a few steps away from Longarm.

"Kill the gringo!" screamed Ortiz.

Longarm figured some of the cowboys from the saloon might come to his aid, since punchers in town in the middle of the day were likely bored and would welcome a fight to sort of liven things up. But none of them did, and he wondered just how buffaloed Ortiz had the whole town. Maybe they were all scared of him for some reason. Longarm didn't put much stock in that witch-man business, but maybe the citizens of Rockport did, especially those of the Mexican persuasion. There were more of them crowding around him now with hostile faces, and he was afraid he might wind up having to shoot some of them.

His boss up in Denver, Chief Marshal Billy Vail, wouldn't take kindly to it if he heard that Longarm had gunned some otherwise-innocent civilians who'd gotten carried away and joined a mob. However, Billy would be even more displeased if Longarm allowed said mob to stomp the hell out of him and maybe even kill him. That would put a definite crimp in the job Longarm had been sent here to do. So he flipped the Colt around the right way and got ready to send a warning shot over the heads of the crowd, hoping that would bring them back to their senses.

Before Longarm could squeeze the trigger, a louder, heavier blast roared out. The crowd fell back and moved away from him, and a tall, gangling, stick figure of a man moved through the opening that had been created. He held a shotgun in his hands, one barrel of which was still smoking. "What in blazes is goin' on here?" he demanded. Then his angry gaze fell on El Pollo. "Oh, hell. I should'a knowed you'd have somethin' to do with this trouble, Ortiz."

The little dandy crossed his arms again and glowered at the newcomer. "This is none of your concern, Sheriff," he informed the shotgun-wielder in a haughty tone of voice. "It is a matter of honor. This man interfered with my servants."

The newcomer, who had a law badge pinned to a black-and-white cowhide vest, looked at Longarm and asked, "Who're you?"

"Deputy United States Marshal Custis Long," Longarm said, not holstering his gun just yet even though the sheriff was looking at it sort of balefully. "Sorry for the ruckus, Sheriff, but I was just trying to help out a lady."

The sheriff looked at Ortiz and asked, "You ain't got Hector chasin' down *señoritas* for you again, have you, Ortiz?"

"It is an honor to serve El Pollo," Ortiz sniffed.

"I ain't goin' to argue about that, but this here is the U.S. of A., not Mexico, and you can't just go around grabbin' gals and makin' 'em wait on you hand and foot. I've told you about this before." The sheriff sounded more weary than angry now.

Ortiz was getting red in the face, reminding Longarm of a boil that was about ready to pop. "I am the *brujo!*" he shouted.

"Yes, sir, you surely are. But I think you best take Hector and these boys of yours and move on. There's been enough trouble for one day. I don't like guns goin' off around here."

Ortiz leveled a finger at Longarm. "This gringo is the one who fired."

"I know that, and I'll speak to him about it. Now you run along."

For a moment Longarm thought Ortiz was going to have a stroke right then and there, but the little man settled for pointing a finger at him and spitting out another string of Spanish. Longarm caught part of it, enough to understand why the Mexicans in the crowd—and some of the Anglos—drew back hurriedly. The girl Hector had been chasing made the sign of the cross, her lips moving in a silent prayer as if to ward off evil.

Longarm just smiled at Ortiz. "Well, old son, I reckon I've been cursed *at* more'n my share, but this is the first time somebody's gone and put a curse *on* me."

"You will regret your interference, gringo," Ortiz snarled. "You will rue the day you set eyes on El Pollo!"

"I already do. Now, didn't you hear the sheriff? Scat!"

Ortiz jerked his head at his men, then turned and stalked off. The others followed him, led by the giant Hector.

The sheriff lowered his shotgun and used one hand to scratch a lean jaw stubbled with a graying beard. "Well, Marshal Long, I reckon you done stepped in it," he said. "Ortiz ain't the kind to forgive and forget."

"You mean that curse he put on me?" Longarm laughed and holstered his gun. "I'm afraid of a lot of things, Sheriff, but

10

a mad little Mexican banty rooster spitting words at me ain't one of 'em." He extended his hand toward the local lawman.

The sheriff grunted and shook hands briefly, then introduced himself. "Name's Tim Packer. You here in Rockport on business, Marshal?"

"That's right."

"Reckon I've got an idea what it's about. You want to come over to the office and fill me in on it?"

"I'll sure do that," Longarm promised, "but not right now. I want to make sure that gal gets home all right." He looked around for the girl who had been fleeing from Hector. She stood a few feet away, smiling shyly and moving the toes of one bare foot around in the dust.

"You all right, Blanca?" the sheriff asked her.

She nodded. "*Sí*, Sheriff Packer. I fear that El Pollo will send Hector after me again, though."

"Probably not anytime soon," Packer said. "You'd best keep your eyes open."

"*Sí*, I intend to do this."

"I'll walk you home, ma'am," Longarm volunteered. "Your name's Blanca?"

"*Sí*. I will feel much better if you come with me, Señor Long."

Longarm glanced at the sheriff. "That all right with you?"

Packer shrugged. "Sure. No reason it wouldn't be. To tell you the truth, I don't really trust Ortiz either."

Blanca caught hold of Longarm's arm. "And I so wish for to thank you," she said.

"Well, that ain't necessary," he told her. "I didn't like ol' Hector nearly running over me like he did. Wasn't much of a welcome."

"I hope your next welcome will be a much more pleasant one, *señor*." Blanca's eyes drooped even more.

Longarm looked at Packer and grinned. The sheriff just shook his head, tucked the shotgun away under his arm, and pointed down the street. "Don't forget to stop by my office once you, ah, get Blanca safely home."

"I'll sure do that."

The crowd had broken up and gone on about its business, and no one paid much attention as Longarm linked arms with Blanca and started down the street with her, letting her lead the way. She kept chattering about how grateful she was, and he let her go on until he started feeling a mite embarrassed at the praise she was heaping on his head. He asked, "Does that fella Ortiz do things like this very often? Have Hector grab gals to be slaves for him, I mean?"

"At least once a month a young woman is forced into servitude," Blanca replied.

"What the hell does he do with them? And why does the law put up with it?"

"The families of the girls do not wish to make El Pollo angry. They fear he will call down the wrath of the spirits on them."

"Like he did with me."

Blanca nodded. "That is right. He has very powerful magic at his command."

Longarm didn't point out the sheer unreasonableness of that belief. When it came to superstition, arguing with folks was usually like trying to whittle down a redwood with a penknife. You might get somewhere eventually, but it would take a damned long time and not be worth the trouble.

"Besides," Blanca added, "the girls are always returned unharmed."

"Well, relatively speaking, I imagine."

She shook her head. "No, no. El Pollo has no interest in them that way. The ones who are virgins when they are taken are returned as virgins. He wishes only for them to serve him and take part in his rituals."

"Then how come you were so desperate to get away?"

"I want no part of the things he does," she said with a shudder. "He is an evil man. He . . . he kills chickens and scatters their feathers and blood around his altar. Some whisper that he sometimes sacrifices other things besides chickens."

"But that's how he got his name, eh?" grunted Longarm.

"Well, he sounds like a mighty unpleasant fella, all right. I can see why you didn't want anything to do with him. How do your folks feel about it?"

Again that calculated shy look toward the ground. "I have no family," Blanca said softly. "I live alone."

"Oh," Longarm said.

"In fact, we are here."

While they had been talking, they had also been walking down a side street into an area of shacks and huts on the edge of Rockport. Longarm saw that they had paused in front of a small frame cottage with a walk of crushed seashells leading to the front door. It was a little more substantial than a shack, without being fancy by any stretch of the imagination.

"This is my home," Blanca said. "You will come in, won't you, Señor Long?"

"Well, I reckon I'd better, just to make sure that Ortiz and Hector ain't hiding inside."

"They would not dare, knowing that you are now my protector."

"I wouldn't be so sure about that." Longarm wanted to point out that he hadn't signed up to look after her from now on either, but she was feeling mighty grateful at the moment and he didn't want to put a dent in that.

She led him inside into a neat little sitting room. Longarm wondered how she afforded a place like this, and as if she was reading his mind, she said, "I am not a *puta,* if that is what you are thinking, Señor Long." She touched the long skirt she wore, which was covered with fancy, colorful embroidery. "I am the, how do you say, seamstress to many of the wealthy ladies in town."

Longarm nodded. "I see. Well, it's obvious you do good work." He gestured toward the skirt as Blanca closed the door of the cottage. "I'm no expert on such things, but that's as pretty a piece of sewing as I've seen in a long time."

"You really think so?" She put her hands on the waistband of the skirt. "Perhaps you would like to take a closer look at it."

13

Before he could stop her, she had pushed the skirt down and wiggled right out of it. That left her smooth brown legs bare. The square-cut hem of her blouse hung down far enough to play hide-and-seek with the thick black hair between her thighs as she strode boldly toward Longarm and held the skirt out to him. Not knowing what else to do, he took it.

"Mighty pretty," he said, his voice a little strained, as he ran his fingertips over the intricate needlework.

"The skirt . . . or me?" Blanca asked. She turned for his inspection, and the bottom half of her rear end was visible under the blouse too. The half-moons of firm, honey-colored flesh contrasted prettily with the white of the blouse.

Longarm smiled at her as she looked back at him over her shoulder. "I reckon I can honestly say this skirt, pretty as it is, can't hold a candle to you, Blanca."

She laughed, grasped the bottom of the blouse, and peeled it up and over her head, giving him a view of her smooth back. Nude, she turned around to face him again. "I am so grateful for what you did to help me, Señor Long."

Longarm's eyes roved over the full breasts with their erect, dark brown tips, the belly with just a hint of pleasant rounding, the flare of her hips and the lush but strong-looking thighs. His shaft had started stiffening as soon as she took off her skirt, and now as he studied the beautiful body she so unashamedly revealed to him, he was rapidly growing uncomfortably hard. But still he was able to say, "You don't have to do this just to say thank you, Blanca. The words are enough if that's what you want."

"I told you I was no *puta*," she said huskily as she came closer to him. "But I am a woman, and to do this is what I want, Señor Long. It is what I need."

"Well, I've always said a lady should have whatever she wants or needs," Longarm murmured as he leaned over to brush his lips against hers.

It was sort of awkward, what with Blanca naked as a jaybird and him still fully dressed, so they took care of that problem over the next few minutes. Longarm took the Ingersoll watch

14

out of one vest pocket and moved it to the other so that he wouldn't have to pull out the derringer attached to the other end of the heavy gold chain in place of a regular fob. Even with somebody he trusted for the most part, like he did Blanca, he didn't like advertising the presence of the derringer. It had gotten him out of more than one tight spot when he was able to take someone by surprise with it.

That done, he let her pretty much have her way after that, and she didn't waste any time getting him out of his vest, shirt, boots, and trousers. As she peeled down the bottoms of the summer-weight long underwear—all he wore under his clothes at this time of year, especially on jobs that took him to places like Texas that were hotter than the hinges of Hades— his erection sprang free, and she gave a small, happy moan as she took hold of it with both hands. "I see that I will have even more reason to be grateful to you," she said with a sly smile.

Since she was already kneeling in front of him, she leaned forward and opened her mouth, teasing the tip of his shaft with her tongue for a moment before closing her lips around it. She spoke French mighty fluently, Longarm discovered over the next few minutes, before he took hold of her shoulders and pulled her up into his arms.

"You got a bed in this place?" he growled.

"In here," Blanca said breathlessly. She took his hand and led him through a doorway into the bedroom. The bed was an old four-poster with a corn-shuck mattress. She put her hands on his broad chest, rubbing her palms over the thick mat of brown hair, and pushed him back so that he reclined on the mattress. As she swung a leg over him, she declared, "I will do the work. You lie there and enjoy yourself, Señor Long."

"I reckon under the circumstances"—Longarm caught his breath as she took hold of him and settled down on him, his manhood sliding smoothly into her hot, moist sheath—"you ought to start calling me Custis."

"Sí, Custis," she whispered as she leaned forward so that her breasts fell naturally into his palms. Her hips began thrusting back and forth. She caught her bottom lip between her teeth

15

and gasped, "I did not know you would fill me so!"

Longarm began moving too, lifting his hips to meet her every time she plunged down. He kneaded the soft flesh of her breasts and thumbed her insistent nipples. She panted as she rocked on top of him, her movements becoming more and more frantic. She threw her head back and closed her eyes, and a moment later a scream came from her mouth as every muscle in her body tensed and held for what seemed like a long time, then relaxed in a series of trembling little guivers. She slumped forward and rested her head against his chest until she had caught her breath. Then she lifted her face to his and kissed him again, her tongue exploring his mouth in a sensual, lingering search. When she finally took her lips away from his, she whispered, "So good . . . so good. . . . But you did not—"

"Not yet," Longarm told her.

And with that he started to move once more, his arms embracing her tightly as he drove up into her again and again. She gasped, "Again so soon . . . I will die!"

"I never loved a woman to death yet," Longarm told her.

She looked down at him, her eyes smoky and passionate. "Try," she whispered, then pressed her lips to his and plunged her tongue into his mouth again.

Chapter 3

"This is a damned strange assignment, Longarm, even if I do say so myself," Billy Vail had told his top deputy a few days earlier in Denver. "So naturally, I thought of you."

Longarm settled back in the morocco leather chair in front of the chief marshal's desk and snapped a lucifer into life with an iron-hard thumbnail. As he held the flame to the tip of the cheroot clenched between his teeth, he said dryly, "Thanks . . . I think."

"You may not thank me when you hear what I've got for you. You're going to Texas."

"Been there many a time," Longarm said. "Hot in the summer, like now, but otherwise it ain't too bad. What part of Texas?"

"The coastline, down along the Gulf of Mexico."

"What's going on down there that's of interest to the Justice Department?"

"Well, actually we're just doing a favor for another government agency. You ever hear of the Karankawa Indians?"

Longarm suppressed a groan and answered the question with one of his own. "This is another one of them BIA chores, ain't it?"

"Well, it's not my fault that you've done such a good job

whenever they asked you to help out in the past," Vail snapped.

It was true that Longarm had handled several previous assignments at the request of the Bureau of Indian Affairs, and most of them had come to satisfactory conclusions . . . but not without a heap of trouble and bloodshed along the way. He puffed on the cheroot for a moment, blew smoke in the direction of the banjo clock on the wall, and said, "No, I don't recollect hearing of any Karankawa Indians. What sort are they?"

"Cannibal," Vail said.

Longarm leaned forward. "Beg your pardon, Billy. I thought I heard you say these here Indians you mentioned are cannibals. That can't be right."

"The hell it can't," Vail said. "I suppose I should say they *were* cannibals. Between the muskets and the diseases the Spaniards brought with 'em when they started colonizing Texas, most of the Karankawas died out. The few surviving members of the tribe disappeared about forty years ago, and nobody knows what happened to them. There's speculation they may have wandered down to Mexico."

"Sounds like good riddance to me," muttered Longarm. "I've never held much with eating other folks."

"Well, usually they'd just cut out the heart of a fallen enemy and roast it. They believed that would give them the strength of the warrior they'd killed. Every now and then, they'd take a fella's liver too."

"Man gets tired of eating the same thing all the time," Longarm said. "I still don't see what the hell this has got to do with us."

Vail regarded Longarm solemnly. "It looks like the Karankawas might have come back to Texas."

Longarm raised an eyebrow quizzically. "Do tell? What happened, Billy, they find some ol' boy with his heart cut out and ate down there in Texas?"

"Yep." Vail nodded. "Two of them, in fact."

Longarm's eyes widened in surprise. "Now, Billy, you wouldn't be joshing me, would you?" he asked.

Vail picked up a couple of sheets of paper and thrust them across the desk toward Longarm. "It's all here in this report the BIA wired me. You can read it for yourself."

For the next few minutes, Longarm did so, scanning the pages that told how two men had been found murdered in the vicinity of St. Charles Bay, near the towns of Fulton and Rockport. Longarm had never been there, but he had visited Corpus Christi, a good-sized seaport town about thirty-five miles south along the gulf coast. The two dead men had been identified as Red Carswell and Alonzo Tarrant, itinerant sailors whose last known addresses were both at a seaman's boardinghouse in Corpus Christi. According to the local law, both Carswell and Tarrant had been beaten to death, but both men also had gaping knife wounds in their chests—and no heart. The ashes of small fires had been found near the dead men, leading to speculation that their hearts had been carved out, roasted, and eaten, since no other sign of the hearts themselves had been found. Longarm frowned and tossed the sheets of paper back onto Vail's desk.

"Mighty grisly stuff," he commented. "But is it enough for the BIA to get up in arms about some so-called man-eating Indians who haven't even been around for forty years?"

Vail replied, "The BIA didn't get involved until the local population down there got wind of what had happened and started spreading rumors about the Kronks coming back. That's what the Karankawas were called, by the way—Kronks. Folks up and down the coast are worried that more people are going to be killed and cannibalized."

"So I get to go down there and straighten things out before those scared locals start stringing up anybody they find with an all-over sunburn, whether they're some of these Kronks or not."

"That's about the size of it," Vail said with a nod. "Find out if the Karankawas have really come back, and if they have, whether or not they're responsible for murdering those two sailors. If they're not, I reckon you'll just have to find the real killers."

"Yeah, I can see why you thought of me when this case hit your desk, Billy," Longarm said with a humorless grin. "Sounds like it's right up my alley."

"That's what I thought," Vail agreed in complete seriousness. "Pick up your travel vouchers and expense money from Henry. He ought to have everything ready for you by now."

Longarm picked up his hat from the floor beside the chair and stood up. "Want me to bring you back a souvenir from Texas?" he asked. "How about a nice heart? One that's a good roasting size."

"Just do me a favor," Vail said disgustedly. "Don't leave *your* heart down there."

Longarm grinned and went into the outer office. Vail's clerk and typewriter jockey, a pale young man named Henry with whom Longarm had developed a grudging friendship, handed him the packet of vouchers and money that would take him from Denver to the gulf coast of Texas. "Who are you after this time, Longarm?" Henry asked. "Pirates?"

"Nope. Cannibals. Big, ugly cannibal Indians."

Henry frowned. "You're joking, surely."

Longarm shook his head and said, "Never been more serious in my life."

"Cannibals," Henry said with a shudder. "You'd better be careful, Longarm."

"Hell, don't worry about me, Henry. I'm too old and stringy for any self-respecting cannibal to eat. They'd have to boil me in a pot for a week to soften me up enough. Anyway, all these particular heathens do is carve out your heart and cook it over a fire. They leave practically all the meat on the bones."

"Please," Henry said, holding up a hand to stop Longarm. "I just ate lunch not that long ago."

"Who did you . . . I mean, what did you have, Henry? Tasty, was it?"

Henry just gave him a baleful look and shooed him out of the office. Longarm went back to his rented room to pack the few belongings he would take with him on this job, pondering as he did so just why none of the other deputies ever got this kind of case. . . .

If he had been able to stay on the same train, the trip to Texas might have taken only a couple of days. But after leaving town on the Denver & Rio Grande, he switched to the Rock Island line at Raton, stayed with it to Fort Worth, picked up the Missouri Pacific there, transferred to the Katy System in Waco, went back to the Missouri Pacific for the run from Taylor to San Antonio, then finished up by taking the Southern Pacific from the Alamo city to Corpus Christi— which meant "Body of Christ." The settlement on the shores of Nueces Bay had been growing in importance ever since being founded in the forties as a trading post. Now it was a port of call for ships from all over the world. It was a pretty place too, with lots of tall trees and nice houses along the waterfront, but after all the switching back and forth from railroad to railroad and dozing on hard wooden benches in assorted depots while he waited for the next train, Longarm was tired and glad to see Corpus Christi only because it signified the end of a journey that had taken twice as long as it should have.

Of course, the trip wasn't really over, either. From Corpus he had ridden a ferry across Nueces Bay to the town of Ingleside, and there had caught a stagecoach that ran through Aransas Pass and up to Rockport. That was where he had disembarked from the stage and wound up on the wrong end of a big Mexican's fist, setting off the chain of events that had led him to have a curse put on his head for the first time in his life.

And it had led him into Blanca's bed, too, he recalled now as he puffed contentedly on a cheroot and stared sleepily up at the ceiling of the bedroom. Blanca was stretched out beside him, her nude body cuddled next to his in the curve of his arm. She was sleeping soundly, her lips curved slightly in the smile of a satisfied woman. Longarm hadn't loved her to death—not quite—but they had sure worn each other out.

Longarm needed to get up, get dressed, and get himself down to Sheriff Packer's office. It was standard procedure for a deputy marshal to check in officially with the local law when working on a case, and besides, he wanted to ask the sheriff about the murders of the two sailors. Packer might have some information that hadn't made it into the report sent to Billy Vail's office by the Bureau of Indian Affairs.

But in the heat of late afternoon, it was much easier just to lie there and lazily stroke the smooth warm skin of Blanca's back, so that's what Longarm did. She sighed in her sleep and snuggled even closer to him as his fingers reached the cleft between her buttocks and traced the upper end of that valley. Her wiggling became more intense as he searched a little further.

Then her eyes opened and she breathed an endearment in Spanish. She reached over and wrapped her fingers around his manhood, which was perking up right nicely again. The warmth of her palm as she slid it up and down brought him fully erect again.

Longarm didn't wait for her to wake up completely. He rolled her onto her back and moved over her, and her thighs parted instinctively. She grasped his shaft and placed in position so that one strong surge of his hips sent it sliding through her portals. Longarm launched into the age-old rhythm as she clasped arms and legs around him and drew his face down to hers.

Longarm kept up the pace for several minutes, bringing both of them closer and closer to the peak. Blanca was gasping and panting and moaning as she tossed her head from side to side. Longarm figured he was making some racket himself, but if he was he couldn't hear it over the blood pounding in his head. Blanca grabbed him even tighter and let out a howl, and he felt himself sliding faster and faster toward the edge.

That was when something plopped down in the middle of his back, the impact so light that he barely felt it in his distracted state.

But he sure as hell felt it a second later when a white-hot knife blade plunged into his skin.

Actually, it just hurt like a white-hot knife blade, Longarm discovered as he yelled out a curse and flipped over like a flapjack on a sizzling griddle. He pawed at his agonized back with one hand while lunging for the holstered revolver on the bedside table with the other. His fingers closed around the butt of the revolver and jerked it free. But there was no enemy to be seen. The room was empty except for Longarm and Blanca.

Not quite, he realized as he saw the small shape scuttling along the sheet toward Blanca's hip. Blanca was still panting as she stared in confusion at Longarm. She must have thought he had gone mad.

He was mad, all right. Mad as hell at the scorpion that had dropped off the ceiling onto his back and stung him. He snapped at Blanca, "Be still," then reached over and used the barrel of the Colt to flick the nasty-looking varmint out of the bed. It sailed through the air and landed on the floor. Longarm went after the little venom-packing son of a bitch, leaning out of the bed as he reversed the pistol. The scorpion, which was about two inches long through the body, with a wicked barbed tail almost that long curved above it, seemed to be staring up at him defiantly, even though Longarm knew that was crazy. It was as if the thing was daring him to seek revenge on it for the sting.

"Bastard," Longarm muttered as he brought the butt of the gun down on the scorpion, crushing it with a small crunching sound. He stared in distaste at the scorpion guts left on the butt of the gun as he lifted it.

"Custis, you are all right?" Blanca asked anxiously as he sat up.

"Yeah. But that's one scorpion that won't ever sting nobody again."

"*El escorpion?* Let me see." She examined his back and winced. Longarm couldn't see the place, of course, but from the way it felt, the scorpion's stinger had left behind a big red welt. The pain was easing a bit already, however, and Longarm had been stung by enough of the critters to know that unlike some people, he didn't have a violent reaction to the venom. It hurt like blazes at the time and left a place that would be sore for a day or two, but he knew he could shrug off the discomfort of it.

"I'll be all right," Longarm assured the young woman. He even managed to chuckle a little as he went on. "I wish the little dickens had waited a few minutes before he decided to fall on me like that. Can't get over the way he was looking at me before I killed him, almost like he was laughing at me."

Blanca's mouth fell open, and she breathed, "El Pollo!"

"What?" Longarm asked with a frown. "You're not talking about that silly curse, are you?"

"El Pollo sent that *escorpion* after you," Blanca declared, fear shining in her eyes. "I am sure of it! He can command all the vile creatures of the earth!"

"Like that fella Hector," Longarm muttered. "But really, Blanca, you can't believe that Ortiz sent that scorpion to sting me just as we were . . . well . . ."

"I know he did. It is the curse of El Pollo!" She hugged herself like it was suddenly cold in the room, despite the muggy heat that would linger until long after dark. "I think you should go, Custis."

"If that's what you want," he said rather stiffly, a trifle offended that she would run him off over something like a scorpion sting and some posturing by a ridiculous little man.

"No, no, you do not understand. You should leave Rockport. Leave Texas if you can. Go far away, so far that the curse of El Pollo can no longer reach you."

"How far you reckon I'd have to go before that curse runs out of steam?"

"I do not know. But you must leave. It is your only chance."

"I can't," Longarm said as he stood up and reached for his pants. "My boss sent me down here to do a job of work, and I got to do it if it's in my power." He continued getting dressed as Blanca watched him worriedly.

"You will not go back where you came from?" she asked as he picked up his Stetson.

"Nope. I'm going down to the sheriff's office to talk to him about the case that brought me here."

"Then I will light a candle for you and say a prayer, tonight and every night. You will need all the prayers you can get if you are to survive the curse."

Longarm leaned over the bed and kissed her lightly on the lips, putting a hand under her chin and tilting her head up to do so. "I generally take all the help I can get," he told her gently. "So you be sure and say those prayers. Now I got to go visit a spell with Sheriff Packer."

As he left the room, she called after him, "Come back to see me again, Custis . . . if you can."

"Count on it," he told her.

Chapter 4

Longarm found the sheriff's office on a side street in Rockport, a few blocks from the harbor. The smell of dead fish that was so common all along the gulf coast hung over the town, mixed with the faint, lingering scent of cow shit. This area had been a major shipping point for cattle from the ranches inland in south Texas, Longarm recalled, before the ranchers had started driving their herds north along the great overland cattle trails to Kansas. Immediately after the Civil War, several rendering plants had been built in the area too, boiling cow carcasses down for their tallow. That left a peculiar stench of its own. Underlying everything else was a hint of sulphur, and Longarm knew from previous visits to this part of the country not to drink the water. It tasted like hell from all the minerals in it.

Well, he thought, that was a good excuse to confine his drinking to some good Maryland rye, if he could find some.

But first he had to drop in on Sheriff Packer, whose office was on the first floor of a boxlike wooden building. Longarm saw bars on the windows of the second floor and figured that was the cell block up there.

The sheriff wasn't alone when Longarm came into the office. A middle-aged man and woman stood in front of the desk, both of them talking at once and sounding agitated as all get-out.

26

Packer let them babble for a few seconds, then held up his hands and said firmly, "Hold on there. I can figure out that your girl's missin', but other than that I ain't makin' much sense out of this. Why don't you just settle down, Mrs. Williams, and let Ben tell me about it."

The woman started sobbing then, and the man put his arm around her shoulders and held her tightly. Longarm figured them for husband and wife. He crossed his arms and leaned against the wall just inside the door as the man said, "We're at our wits' end, Sheriff Packer. We come home earlier today from visitin' Alma's folks up in Refugio, and when we got back Stella was gone, just gone."

Packer leaned back in his chair and looked sympathetic. "I'm tryin' to remember," he said. "How old's Stella now?"

"She's sixteen, Sheriff, just sixteen."

After a moment's hesitation, Packer grimaced and said, "Now don't take offense at this, Ben, but is it possible she could've run off on her own? Say with a young fella?"

The woman let out another big sob, and Williams shook his head. "I almost wish that's the way it was," he said. "But Stella ain't had nobody courtin' her serious-like."

"She's a pretty girl," Packer pointed out.

"Yes, sir, I know. But she's a good church-goin', God-fearin' girl too, and she wouldn't run off with no boy. No, Sheriff, that ain't it, we're sure. Besides, she didn't take nothin' with her, no clothes and none of her other things. She would've taken something with her if she was runnin' off with a boy, wouldn't she?"

"You'd think so," Packer muttered, looking more unhappy than ever. "You talk to any of your neighbors, Ben?"

"That's the first thing we did. Thought she might've been visitin' somebody. But nobody had seen her, and nobody saw anything funny goin' on around the house, neither. It's like she just up and vanished into thin air, Sheriff!"

"That ain't possible." Packer glanced over at Longarm, then returned his attention to his other visitors. "Tell you what, Ben. You take the missus on home, and I'll be over there directly

27

to take a look around and ask the neighbors some questions of my own. Could be somebody's remembered something by now that'll help us. I'll go by the telegraph office, too, and wire the authorities in the surrounding counties to be on the lookout for a gal answerin' Stella's description. That's about all I can do right now."

"You've got to find her, Sheriff!" Alma Williams wailed. "You've just got to. She's our only baby!"

Packer stood up and hurried around the desk to pat the distraught woman on the shoulder. "Now, now, don't you worry about a thing, ma'am. We'll get your little girl back, I promise you."

Williams managed to shepherd his sobbing wife out of the office, and Packer called after them, "I'll be over there in just a little while." Then he closed the door, turned to Longarm, and said, "Well, if it ain't the federal law. You get Blanca home all right?"

"She's fine," Longarm said. "Didn't see any more sign of that fella Ortiz or that big gent called Hector." He left out any mention of how Blanca had expressed her gratitude to him, as well as the incident with the scorpion.

"Blanca's a nice little gal, does quite a bit of sewing for my wife. I wouldn't want you gettin' the wrong idea about her, Marshal. She ain't no whore."

"Don't worry, Sheriff, she made that plain as day." Longarm picked up a chair and reversed it, then said, "Mind if I sit down? I know you're busy, but I won't take up too much of your time."

"Help yourself," Packer said as he went behind the desk and sat down again.

Longarm straddled the chair and thumbed back his hat, then took out a cheroot. He offered it to the sheriff, who shook his head. Then he scratched a lucifer into life and lit it himself. "Those folks who were just in here sound like they've got themselves a problem."

"Yeah, and so have I. Stella Williams is a flighty little thing, and even though Ben and Alma can't believe she'd run off, it

28

don't seem so far-fetched to me, 'specially if there was a boy involved. Young gals can get some mighty peculiar notions in their heads where romance is concerned."

"Maybe the Kronks got her," Longarm suggested with a grin.

Packer glowered at him. "Don't you say such a thing out loud around here. I already got folks scared to death they're goin' to be jumped by some savage bent on cuttin' their heart out if they dast step outside their house. I figured it was the Kronks what brought you to town, Marshal Long. Or them two murders ever'body's blamin' on the Kronks, I should say."

"Call me Longarm; most folks do. And you're right, I'm down here investigating those killings on behalf of the Justice Department, which is doing a favor for the Bureau of Indian Affairs. Seems the BIA doesn't want the Kronks blamed unfairly, as well as wanting to find out if there even *are* any Kronks left. Reckon you could shed some light on that for me, Sheriff?"

"Wish I could," Packer said with a sigh. "I been over and over the ground where them bodies were found, and I didn't come up with a thing except a bunch of footprints so jumbled up you couldn't tell nothin' from 'em."

"Footprints of men wearing boots?" asked Longarm.

Packer shrugged. "Hard to say. Some of 'em could've been made by bare feet. You're thinkin' that if it was savages responsible for the murders, they wouldn't have been wearin' shoes?"

"The thought crossed my mind," Longarm allowed. "What about the places the bodies were found?"

"Close to the bay, not right on the beach but within fifty yards of it. The men were found about a half mile apart, Carswell a week ago, Tarrant a week before that."

Longarm mused, "A week between killings, eh? That'd mean another one's about due if there's any sort of pattern to it."

"Lord, I hope not!" Packer said fervently. "We get our share of shootin's and knifin's around here, what with so many sailors and cowboys around, but the thought of a regular cold-blooded murder ever' week gives me the fantods."

"Well, maybe there ain't nothing to that idea," Longarm said. "What about the dead men themselves? You know anything about them?"

Packer shook his head and said, "Just their names and that they were sailors. They lived down in Corpus when they weren't at sea. Both of 'em were identified by sailors who'd shipped out with 'em in the past, although not recently."

Longarm digested that information for a moment, then asked, "I suppose there's no chance the BIA made a mistake in their report when they said the corpses were missing their hearts?"

A shudder ran through Packer. "I seen 'em both," he declared. "Their hearts were gone, all right. The coroner hereabouts is our undertaker, Desmond Yantis, and he said the same thing after he examined the bodies. Havin' their hearts missin' would be strange enough, but when word got out about the ashes of those cookfires bein' found close by the bodies . . . well, it was just too much for folks. They started talkin' about how the Karankawas had come back, and I ain't been able to stifle that talk yet."

"You give any thought to calling in the Rangers?" Longarm had worked both with and against the Texas Rangers in the past, and despite his occasional differences with them, he knew them to be more than capable when it came to law enforcement.

"I sent word to Austin, but McNelly's Special Force is busy down along the border tryin' to corral some Mexicans who been raidin' across the Rio, and Major Jones has got his hands full out West, too, what with some Apaches still raisin' hell in the Big Bend. A couple of murders is pretty small potatoes to those boys. They've promised to send a man when they can, but who knows when that'll be."

"Well, I'll do what I can to make sure they ain't needed," Longarm said. He put his hands on the back of the chair and started to stand up.

Packer stopped him by saying, "You're not the only one who's interested in the Kronks, you know. There's a stranger here in town askin' all sorts of questions about 'em."

Longarm settled back down on the chair and looked interested. "A stranger, eh? Got any idea who he is?"

"She," said Packer. "It's a woman."

A small frown of surprise appeared on Longarm's forehead. Why would a woman be poking around Rockport, asking questions about a bunch of cannibal Indians? Somehow that didn't seem decent to him.

"Well, do you know who she is?" he demanded.

"Says her name's Miss Nora Ridgley, and I can tell by her accent she's from back East somewhere. Couldn't tell you where, though, or why she's so interested in the Kronks. I thought maybe you'd know."

Longarm shook his head. "I never heard of her before. I may have to have a talk with her, though. I don't want to go tripping over any civilian while I'm having a look around."

"She's stayin' at the Rockport House," Packer said. "That's the best hotel in town, right down on the water. You can't miss it."

"Thanks, Sheriff." This time Longarm managed to stand up without hearing anything surprising enough to make him sit down again. "I reckon my bag's still over at the stage station. I sort of lost track of it during that ruckus with Ortiz and his boys."

"If you left it there, it'll still be there. The station manager takes good care of things like that." Packer stood up too, and reached for his hat. "Reckon I'd better head on over to the Williams house and look around a mite, like I promised. You stay in touch, hear?"

"I'll do that," Longarm promised. "Thanks for your help, Sheriff Packer." He grinned broadly. "You being a lawman and all, I reckon that makes you a star Packer, don't it?"

The sheriff regarded him stonily. "That was right funny . . . the first five hundred times I heard it. Sort of like you must

31

really enjoy bein' kidded about bein' the long arm of the law."

"You get used to it," Longarm said with a chuckle. "See you later, Sheriff."

He stepped outside and turned one way, toward the harbor, while Packer followed him out and then turned the other way. Longarm waved to the sheriff, then started angling across the street toward the stage station to reclaim his bag.

He was halfway across when a wagon being pulled by a six-horse hitch came around a nearby corner and rolled quickly past him. The hooves of the horses and the wheels of the wagon splashed through a broad mud puddle Longarm had been about to circle around. Mud flew up and splattered his boots and trousers and vest.

Longarm jumped back with an angry curse, but the driver of the wagon never looked behind him at the man he had nearly run over. Of course, he hadn't actually come that close to being run over, Longarm conceded as he started trying to wipe off the mud clinging stickily to his clothes. The wagon had missed him easily, and the only real damage it had done was splashing mud on him. But that was bad enough, Longarm thought disgustedly.

Maybe this was Ortiz's curse working again, making his life miserable. That possibility occurred to him, but he discarded it with a curt shake of his head. He had just had a run of bad luck, first with the scorpion, now with the mud splattered on his clothes. That was all, just some bad luck.

Longarm kept repeating that to himself as he brushed off as much of the mud as possible and went on over to the stagecoach station.

The way things were going, Longarm wouldn't have been surprised if his bag had disappeared from the station, but it was there, just as Packer had said it would be. The station manager complained some about having to retrieve it from the street outside following the disturbance, but he calmed down when Longarm showed him his badge and credentials.

"Glad to be of help, Marshal," the man said after that. "Always glad to do whatever we can for the federal government."

"Don't let anybody in Congress hear you say that," Longarm advised. "They might have more things they want than you'd think was possible."

Picking up his bag, Longarm walked on down the street toward the waterfront. The first man he stopped pointed out the Rockport House to him. It was as fine a place as the sheriff had indicated, a three-story building with a green lawn on all sides, a covered verandah all around the building, and a lot of shrubs and bushes to set things off. The hotel was painted a pale blue that matched the color of the sky pretty well, and its roof was whitewashed wooden shingles. Another walk, made of crushed seashells that were a startling white against the deep green, led across the lawn to the entrance.

Longarm went through a pair of white-painted doors with big windows in them, into a lobby with more windows to let in plenty of light and the sea air. Of course, that air wasn't so fragrant if the wind was blowing from the wrong direction, as it was today, but to even acknowledge such a thing would ruin the atmosphere of the place, Longarm supposed. So he kept his mouth shut about the smell in the air as he went across the hardwood floor of the lobby, past some potted plants and overstuffed armchairs and divans to a counter where a fella in a white suit waited.

"Good afternoon, sir," the man said to Longarm, his eyes flicking down to check out the mud splatters on Longarm's clothes. Some of his practiced affability disappeared. "What can I do for you?"

"I need a place to hang my hat," Longarm said, "as well as a little information about one of your guests."

The second part of that request shook the clerk's professional smile a little more. "We don't make a practice of giving out information concerning our guests, sir. We'll be perfectly happy to rent you a room, however, if you have the necessary funds to pay for it. We have a few vacancies—"

Longarm didn't let him push on past the matter at hand. "I'm a federal lawman," he said as he lowered his bag to the floor and took out the little leather folder containing his bona fides. He showed them to the clerk and went on. "I want to have a talk with a lady who's supposed to be staying here. Her name's Miss Nora Ridgley. What room's she in?"

"Ah . . ." The clerk hesitated, but Longarm's tired, impatient glare was enough to make him cave in. "Miss Ridgley is in room seven. Shall I send a boy up to announce you?"

"I can take care of that myself, soon as I've checked in. *And* I can pay for the room in advance, if you want," he added pointedly.

"Oh, no, Marshal, that won't be necessary. I hope you didn't take offense. It's just that it's the hotel's policy to protect the privacy of our guests."

Longarm waved off the explanation, then signed the register the clerk turned around on the counter for him. "I can put you in room eleven," the man went on. "That's just two doors down from Miss Ridgley's room."

"Much obliged," Longarm told him. He added, "I'll carry my own bag," as the clerk lifted a hand to hit one of those little bells that usually summoned a boy in a suit like an organ-grinder's monkey's. "I'm traveling light."

He got the key and went up a broad staircase to the second floor and then down a hallway, passing room seven on the way to his own room, which turned out to be a cramped chamber with the typical big window, this one overlooking the sea, which washed in on a narrow white beach where little round tables were set up underneath large, brightly colored umbrellas. Folks sat at those tables and sipped drinks as the wind fluttered the tassels that hung down from the edges of the umbrellas. Longarm supposed they thought of themselves as downright elegant for doing so. And it might have been more appealing, he admitted, if the breeze had been blowing in with the clean salt tang of the ocean, rather than coming from inland and carrying the smell of rotting fish.

Leaving the bag containing his jacket, a clean shirt, a razor, and a box of spare .44-40's on the bed, Longarm walked back down the hall to room seven. He hadn't asked the clerk if Miss Nora Ridgley was in her room or not, but it was coming on toward evening and most folks would be getting ready for supper. There was a good chance she was there. Longarm rapped his knuckles on the door.

A few seconds later, a woman's voice asked from the other side, "Who is it?"

"My name's Long, ma'am," Longarm told her. "I'm a lawman, and I'd like to speak to you for a minute, please."

Again there was a brief hesitation, then she said, "All right," and the door swung open. The woman standing just inside asked, "What's the meaning of this, sir? You don't think I'm entertaining a gentleman in my room, do you?"

Longarm took a quick gander at her, and saw she was wearing a silk dressing gown that clung to her enough for him to tell there wasn't a heap of meat on those bones. She wouldn't have made much of a meal for a cannibal Indian if he was interested in anything other than her heart, Longarm thought. Nor was her pale, narrow face particularly attractive, and it was made even less so by the way her straw-colored hair was pulled back so tightly and coiled in a braid around the back of her head.

Longarm tipped a finger to the brim of his Stetson and said, "No, ma'am, that notion never entered my head, and I can see now you ain't the type of lady to do anything so improper." Not that this gal was even going to be able to get a gent in her room without lassoing and hog-tying him, he added to himself. He went on quickly. "My name's Custis Long, and I'm a deputy U.S. marshal. Sheriff Packer tells me you've been asking questions around town about the Karankawas?"

"And what if I have, Marshal?" she returned coolly.

"Well, you see, that's why I'm here, too," he began.

She reached out suddenly and clutched his arm. There was surprising strength in her long, slender fingers. "You've come here to investigate the murders?" she asked.

Longarm nodded. "That's right."

35

"Then you're the man the Bureau sent."

Something about the familiarity with which she mentioned the BIA puzzled Longarm. He said, "Pardon my asking, ma'am, but what do you know about the Bureau?"

She started tugging him into the room. "Come inside," she said as she glanced up and down the hall. "I have a dinner engagement, but I'm sure my friend won't mind waiting a few minutes. We don't want to discuss this out in the open where anyone can hear."

Longarm wasn't sure he wanted to spend much time alone in a room with Miss Nora Ridgley, but she wasn't giving him much choice if he wanted to get to the bottom of her involvement in this case. He let her pull him into the room and then shut the door behind him. She was smiling as she turned to face him again, and while the expression made her a little prettier, it wasn't anything to make him sit up and take notice.

"I've been waiting for another investigator to arrive," she said. "I didn't expect anyone quite so . . . impressive as you, however, Marshal Long. You're rather large and rugged-looking, aren't you?" She crossed her arms over a bosom that could be generously described as sparse and gave him an even bigger smile.

He had heard enough folks from up around Boston to peg her accent as coming from that part of the country. But much more important than how she talked was what she said. "Did you say *another* investigator?" he asked.

"That's right. The Bureau of Indian Affairs sent me here to look into this matter."

Longarm frowned. "Now hold on. That's one too many bites out of the apple. *I'm* here at the request of the BIA. Why would they sent somebody else to poke around in the same case that brought me here?"

"I'm sure I couldn't tell you, Marshal Long. Shall I call you Custis?" Without waiting for him to answer, she went on. "It's not unusual to find duplication of effort within a bureaucracy. I'm sure you've encountered that yourself if you've worked for the government for very long. Often one part of an agency doesn't know what another part is doing, or perhaps they simply don't trust each other to do the job properly. At any rate, we're both here, and I'm looking forward to working with you, Custis. I've already done some preliminary questioning of possible witnesses—"

Longarm held up his hands and practically yelled, "Hold it! Rein in that team, ma'am. I'm afraid you and me won't be working together. You won't be working on this case at all."

She looked like she didn't know whether to be startled or disappointed or angry, so she settled for some of each. "What are you talking about?" she demanded. "Of course we'll be working together. Why shouldn't we?"

"For one thing, I generally work alone. For another, my boss didn't say anything to me about there being a BIA agent down here. He sent *me* to sort out this mess."

"I see," Nora Ridgley said indignantly. "Interdepartmental rivalry. I've seen it before, and it's an ugly thing."

"I don't know about that rivalry business. I've got along just fine with folks who work for other parts of the government, when somebody higher up told me I was supposed to. But right now I don't have any proof that you even work for the BIA, let alone that you've been assigned to this case. Not to put too fine a point on it, I didn't even know the BIA had any women working for it."

She glared at him and said, "If that's a request for me to produce identification papers, I'm afraid I can't. I left them behind in Washington, of course. Or don't you know anything about working undercover, Marshal?"

Well, at least she wasn't calling him Custis anymore, Longarm thought. He supposed that was progress of a sort. He said, "I know enough not to want to find myself tripping over somebody who's got no business being there while I'm poking around. So I'll thank you to steer clear of me, Miss Ridgley. In fact, the best thing you could do—if you really work for the BIA—is to go back to Washington and tell your bosses everything's under control down here."

"Is that so? You've solved the case already, Marshal Long? Just how long have you been here in Rockport?"

"Got here a couple of hours ago."

"My, you *are* a fast worker, aren't you?" Sarcasm as thick as molasses dripped from her voice.

Longarm struggled to hang on to his temper as he replied, "No, I don't have anything figured out yet, but I will. And I reckon it'll get solved faster if I don't have to worry about you interfering with me."

"I won't abandon my duty any more than you would, Marshal," she said stubbornly. "I'm afraid you shall just have to tolerate my continued presence. But I will try to avoid troubling you." She gave him a haughty look. "For one thing, tying my investigation to yours might hold me back."

Longarm tightened his jaw and managed not to say anything for a moment. Finally, he nodded curtly and said, "I guess we understand each other, then. Good evening to you, Miss Ridgley."

"Good evening," she said frostily.

He went to the door, put his hand on the knob, and looked back at her rigid, angry figure. "The curse of El Pollo," he muttered.

"What was that?" snapped Nora.

"Nothing," Longarm said. He went out and shut the door behind him, then sighed heavily.

Damned if he wasn't starting to think there might be something to that curse business after all.

Chapter 5

The hotel dining room specialized in seafood, not surprisingly, so Longarm had a plateful of fried whiting and shrimp
and fried potatoes, washed down with a couple of bottles of
beer. The Rockport House also had a bar, so he stopped in
there after he had eaten and found that they stocked Tom
Moore Maryland rye. A couple of shots of the smooth li-
quor made him feel a mite better about things. This assignment might not turn out to be so bad after all. He didn't
often get to stay at a place as fancy as this in the line of
duty.

His good mood was blunted a little as he stepped out of the
bar and saw Nora Ridgley going into the dining room across
the lobby from him. She had her back to him, but he had
no trouble recognizing that skinny figure. She was wearing
a dress of some bottle-green fabric and had a matching hat
perched on her hair, which was still pulled back in that tightly
coiled braid. Nora had mentioned having an engagement for
dinner, and sure enough she was walking arm in arm with
a tall, dark-haired man. Longarm couldn't tell anything else
about him, other than that his suit was well-cut and looked
expensive. He wondered what the gent saw in Nora Ridgley,
then shrugged and told himself that pondering over the whys

and wherefores of romance was just about as time-wasting as trying to teach a pig to sing.

Longarm lit a cheroot in the lobby, then pushed out through the big-windowed front doors and ambled along the walk toward the street. The breeze had turned around since afternoon, and the evening air was a better example of what brought well-to-do folks here to spend their money. It held a hint of coolness along with the crisp scent of the ocean. Longarm drew in a deep breath.

The next morning would be early enough to begin his investigation of the murders. Tonight he was in the mood for a stroll, and without him even thinking about it, his steps turned in the direction of Blanca's cottage. He wanted to make sure she was all right before he turned in. He didn't want Hortensio Ortiz and that big galoot Hector bothering her again.

There were lanterns in the trees on the hotel lawn, casting a bright yellow glow over the grounds so that guests could take an evening constitutional in relative safety. Once Longarm got away from the hotel, though, the number of people he saw moving around declined sharply. Folks were probably staying inside because of the Karankawa scare, he thought.

It took him about a quarter of an hour to walk across Rockport to Blanca's house. When he got there he saw a light in one of the front windows. He dropped the stub of cheroot that was left, crushed it out under his boot heel, and went up the walk to the door. He didn't want to scare Blanca, so as he knocked he called out, "It's me, Blanca, Marshal Long."

The door opened a moment later and she smiled at him in greeting. "Custis, you are back!" she exclaimed.

"Told you I would be."

"And you are . . . all right? Nothing else has happened?"

Longarm knew she was talking about the curse. The mud stains on his pants had dried until they were almost invisible against the brown tweed of his trousers. He decided not to mention that incident—or his run-in with Nora Ridgley. There was no point in feeding Blanca's superstitious fears.

"I'm fine," he told her emphatically. "Don't I look all right?"

"You look very handsome," she said as she stepped back. "Please, come in."

He could tell from the fabric spread out on one side of a little divan that she had been sitting there and working on some sewing. She moved over hurriedly and swept up the material, depositing it on a small side table.

"Please sit down," she said.

Longarm put his Stetson on the table with the fabric and said gallantly, "After you, ma'am."

Blanca smiled again and sat down. Longarm settled on the divan beside her. With that shy expression that was so appealing even though Longarm knew it was calculated, she said, "I have thought a great deal about you. It seems much longer than a few hours since you left. The place on your back where the scorpion stung you . . . it is not too sore?"

Longarm saw a blush creep over her features, and figured she was remembering what they had been doing when the scorpion dropped down from the ceiling to pay a visit. They had never gotten to finish that, he recalled. He said, "It's still a mite sore and will be for a day or two. But it's nothing to worry about. I've been shot and stabbed and bit by wolves and rattlesnakes. A man in my line of work learns to put up with a few aches and pains."

"You are a remarkable man, Custis. I noticed earlier that you have many scars." Her blush deepened.

"All of 'em well-earned," Longarm assured her. "It's been a rough-and-tumble life ever since I came out here to the frontier from West by God Virginia. But I don't reckon I'd trade it."

"You must have known many women."

He nodded and said honestly, "But not many as sweet as you."

She snuggled against him, and his arm sort of went around her natural-like, and it wasn't long before they were kissing. That low-necked peasant blouse of Blanca's got pushed down some way so that her firm breasts were revealed, and one of

41

her pebble-hard nipples found its way into Longarm's mouth. After a few minutes of that, the other one seemed to be demanding equal attention, so Longarm shifted his head about six inches and started using his lips and tongue on the second eager nubbin of flesh. Blanca's hands wound up on the buttons of his trousers, and she proved as deft with them as she was with needle and thread. She freed his erection, pulled up her long skirt, and swung one smooth brown leg to straddle him. She sighed as she sank down to sheath his hardness with her body.

Longarm hoped there weren't any scorpions around tonight. Because if any varmint interrupted this time, he wasn't going to be satisfied with squashing the little son of a bitch. That would be too much of a quick and easy death. Nope, anybody or anything bothering him right about now was going to learn the true meaning of the word *revenge*. . . .

The streets of Rockport were even more deserted when Longarm left Blanca's cottage a couple of hours later and walked back toward the hotel. Their lovemaking had filled him with a pleasant tiredness, and he was looking forward to finding out just how comfortable that bed in his room at the Rockport House really was. At the same time, the part of his brain that was devoted to his work was making plans to rent a horse first thing in the morning and ride up the coast to take a look at the places where the two sailors had died.

That mixture of weariness and anticipation didn't leave as much room as it should have for simply paying attention to his surroundings, and it almost got him killed. He was walking past a row of darkened buildings, stores already closed for the night, when he faintly heard the familiar metallic clicking of a gun's hammer being drawn back.

Longarm threw himself forward as a gun boomed and flame lanced into the night some ten feet to his right. He sensed as much as heard the bullet passing through the air behind his head. One of his boots slipped on the damn seashells that seemed to be underfoot everywhere in this town, and he felt himself falling.

As he fell, he reached across his body and snagged the Colt from the cross-draw rig, then landed on his shoulder and rolled over. Another shot exploded, and this time he felt a flurry of stinging sensations on his face as the bullet plowed into the road next to his head and kicked up a shower of crushed shells. Aiming at the muzzle flash, he triggered the double-action .44 three times as fast as he could.

The revolver bucked in his hand as the shots blasted out. Another gun went off, this one across the street, and Longarm heard the whine as the slug whipped past his head and then thudded into a building. As he rolled over to face the new threat, out of the corner of his eye he saw a dark shape come staggering out of the shadows of what he now realized was a narrow passageway between buildings. There was no time to deal with that, because another man was hurrying across the street toward him, firing on the run. Longarm stayed prone to make himself a smaller target and squeezed off a shot. He didn't think he hit the man charging toward him, but the gent turned tail and ran anyway. It took more courage than most bushwhackers possessed to run straight toward the barrel of a gun.

Longarm came up on one knee and swung toward his original attacker. The man wasn't there anymore. Longarm caught a glimpse of movement over by the corner of one of the buildings and started to trigger off a shot, then held up at the last instant. Better to let a bushwhacker get away than to gun down an innocent bystander, he reminded himself. There was a hell of a lot less paperwork that way, for one thing.

As he got to his feet, Longarm pivoted around in a complete circle, looking for any other sign of trouble. The street seemed to be deserted now except for him. He bent and scooped up his hat, which had fallen off when he went pitching forward, then trotted over to the nearest darkened building and put his back firmly against the wall. Now that nobody could come at him from behind, he clapped his hat on and took a minute to replace the spent shells in the Colt with fresh cartridges from the loops on his gunbelt. He snapped the cylinder closed and stood there waiting to see what was going to happen.

Every dog in town was barking, it seemed, no doubt set off by the gunfire. Longarm listened to the yapping and howling for a few minutes, then decided that the ambushers had well and truly departed. He sidled along the building anyway, keeping to the shadows for the moment.

He hadn't seen the first bushwhacker as anything but a vague shape, but the second man, the hombre who had come charging at him from across the street, had been silhouetted against the faint illumination of the night sky from where Longarm lay on the ground. That look had been enough to tell Longarm that the man had been tall and broad-shouldered. Just downright big, in fact.

About like Ortiz's servant and gal-grabber Hector . . .

Longarm spotted a light coming toward him and recognized it as a bull's-eye lantern. Along with the light came the sound of several curious voices. One of them Longarm recognized as belonging to Sheriff Packer as the local law called out, "All right, what's goin' on down there?"

Holstering his gun, Longarm stepped out into the street away from the building and raised his voice as he replied, "It's Marshal Long, Sheriff."

Packer came up to him, the lantern swinging in one hand, a shotgun tightly gripped in the other. Several men followed Packer, and Longarm figured them for deputies. The sheriff asked, "Was that you doin' all that shootin', Longarm?"

"Only some of it," Longarm told him. "A couple of gents decided to throw some lead in my direction, and since I didn't much want it I threw it back."

Packer grunted. "They catch any of it?"

"I'm pretty sure one did, but he ran off anyway, just like the other fella."

"How about you?"

"I was lucky. Not a scratch."

In the light of the lantern, Packer pointed toward Longarm's face. "Little blood there, on your left cheek."

Longarm touched his cheek, and came away with a faint tinge of red on his fingertips. "One of the bullets hit beside my head and flung up some splinters from those shells in the road. Reckon I've got a scratch or two after all, but nothing to worry about."

Packer turned to his deputies and quickly ordered them to take a look around the area. Longarm didn't think they would find anything; with their mission a failure, the bushwhackers would be long gone.

The sheriff regarded him speculatively and asked, "Now, just who do you think would want to see you killed, Marshal?"

"I can think of one little so-and-so," Longarm replied grimly. "That fella they call El Pollo. Ortiz."

Packer shrugged. "Maybe. Ortiz didn't like how you got his goat this afternoon. Those fellers who work for him, like Hector, generally steer clear of gunplay, though. They might rough somebody up, but they ain't much on bushwhackin'."

"Maybe Ortiz was never that mad at anybody before," suggested Longarm.

"That might be right too. He *was* fit to be tied."

"Where can I find him?" Longarm asked.

Packer frowned at him and said, "You ain't thinkin' of goin' right up to his house, are you?"

"I might," Longarm declared. "I don't much like being shot at. Fact is, it bothers me a hell of a lot more than having a curse put on me."

"Well, I guess I can show you where Ortiz lives," Packer said reluctantly. "You ain't plannin' to shoot up the place, are you? I know you're a federal lawman and all, but Ortiz is a citizen of the county just like anybody else and I got to give him the benefit of the doubt."

"I won't do any shooting unless they force me to," Longarm promised. "Besides, you'll be with me, Sheriff, and if Ortiz really is a law-abiding sort, he won't start any trouble with you there."

45

"All right, come on." Packer lifted the lantern and jerked his head toward the far side of town. As Longarm fell in step beside him, one of the deputies came trotting back to report that they hadn't found anybody suspicious lurking in the vicinity.

"Didn't find anybody, period," the deputy said. "Everybody seems to be locked up tight for the night on account of that Indian scare."

Packer nodded. "Take the boys and go on back to the office," he commanded. "I'll be back after a while."

As they walked along, Longarm asked, "How would you feel about putting out that lantern, Sheriff? It sort of advertises where we are in case anybody wants to take a potshot at us."

"Yeah, you're right," Packer said as he lifted the lantern and blew out the wick. There was still enough light from the moon and stars for them to see where they were going, but if anybody was trying to draw a bead on them, they wouldn't be such good targets now.

Longarm and Packer walked side by side along the practically deserted streets of Rockport until they reached a lane that seemed to be the northwest border of the settlement. Behind them, toward the gulf, lights still burned in quite a few houses, but ahead of them facing inland was darkness.

"There," Packer said, pointing.

Longarm looked where the sheriff was pointing, and after a moment spotted a dark, hulking shape that sprawled out over the flat, brush-dotted landscape. "What the hell's that?" Longarm asked. "Some sort of castle?"

"Damn near. The Spaniards built it a long time ago. How Ortiz got his hands on it I don't know, but he's lived there as long as I've been in this part of the country, which is goin' on fifteen years."

As the two lawmen approached the estate, Longarm could see that there was a high adobe wall built around it. The house itself had at least three stories and was tall enough to loom above the wall. It was adobe too, Longarm figured, with the red tile roof that was so common to the architecture in this part of the world. There was probably a courtyard in the center of the house, with a fountain and maybe some trees growing in it. A gate of intricately wrought black iron closed off the opening in the adobe wall. Packer found a bell pull and yanked on it.

"This fella Ortiz must be rich to live in a place like this," Longarm commented as they waited for someone to respond to the summons.

"Folks pay him to cast spells for them," Packer said. "If you want to ward off evil spirits, or if you want to make somebody fall in love with you or have bad luck happen to one of your enemies, Ortiz is the feller to see."

"You don't believe that hogwash, do you?"

Packer shrugged and said, "It don't matter whether I believe or not. The Mexicans around here do, and to tell the truth, I think a goodly number of the white folks do too. I reckon he does all right for hisself. If he didn't, he couldn't keep this place up."

The heavy wooden door leading into the house swung open, and a figure emerged onto the walk leading across the narrow yard inside the wall. The man came up to the gate and growled, *"Quien es?"*

"Sheriff Packer and Marshal Long," Packer said. "We want to see Señor Ortiz."

"El Pollo has gone to bed," the man said in a thick Mexican accent.

"Well, you'd best wake him up," Longarm advised gruffly, "because I ain't leaving until I've talked to him."

The servant grumbled some and didn't move. Packer shifted the shotgun that was tucked under his arm and said, "We ain't lookin' for trouble, you understand, but we aim to talk to Señor Ortiz. I can go back and fetch some deputies if I have to."

"Wait," the man said curtly. He turned and went back inside the big house.

"Reckon he'll come back out and let us in?" Longarm asked.

"We'll just have to wait and see."

They didn't have to wait long. Three or four minutes went by, and then the servant reappeared. He unlocked the gate with

47

a heavy iron key and swung it open without a word. Longarm and Packer stepped inside, and the man closed the gate behind them. It sounded almost like the door of a prison cell clanging shut, Longarm thought. That wasn't a very comforting notion.

The servant led them inside the house, and escorted them to a high-ceilinged room with thick wooden beams visible along the ceiling. A massive fireplace dominated one wall of the room. Tapestries that Longarm guessed were Mayan hung on two more of the walls. There were soft rugs on the floor, and the furniture was equally opulent. Several small statues, also either Mexican or Central American in origin, were placed on tables around the room. Longarm looked at one of the carvings and said, "Ugly little critter, ain't it?"

"You speak of one of my gods, gringo," a voice said angrily. Hortensio Ortiz strode into the room through another door, his small body wrapped in a silk dressing gown. "Why have you come here to disturb my rest?"

"There was some trouble in town a little while ago," Packer answered. "Somebody took a few shots at Marshal Long here."

Ortiz shrugged and sneered. "I regret only that they seem to have missed. But what affair is this of mine, Sheriff?"

"I was hopin' you could tell us that, Señor Ortiz."

Longarm added, "What the sheriff's getting at is that you might as well admit you sent those hombres after me."

"I did no such thing," Ortiz said indignantly. "I have placed my curse on you, gringo, and that is sufficient for my revenge upon you."

"Yeah, but curses work a heap better when they're backed up with hot lead, don't they, Ortiz?" It took an effort for Longarm to control his temper as he went on. "I got a look at one of the men who ambushed me, and he was about as big as that fella Hector who works for you."

Ortiz glanced over at the servant who had summoned him, a hard-faced Mexican built a lot like Hector, only smaller. The man looked uncomfortable in servant's livery that was a little small on him. A rapid spate of Spanish came from Ortiz's mouth, and the servant answered just as rapidly. Ortiz looked at Longarm and Packer again and said, "Hector has been in his quarters all evening long. He could not have done this thing."

"Even assuming we're going to take your word for that—which we ain't—how do we know you don't have some other bruiser just as big working for you? You'd better check your other servants too; one of 'em's probably carrying some Justice Department lead in him."

"None of my people are injured," Ortiz replied without bothering to ask his majordomo about the matter. "You may see for yourself, although I will not go so far as to say you are welcome to do so."

"We'll take a look around," Packer said mildly.

"Enrique!" snapped Ortiz. "Accompany these . . . men."

The majordomo showed them around the house, including the servants' quarters. Some of Ortiz's men were sleeping and seemed genuinely disturbed when they were awakened. Hector fell into that category. He glared at Longarm with undisguised hatred, but appeared to be honestly surprised to see the federal lawman. A few men were still up playing cards. Without exception, they all insisted they had been on the grounds of the estate all night.

And none of them were wounded, unless they were doing a damned good job of covering it up. Longarm was frowning in frustration as he and Packer returned to the main room, where Ortiz was waiting for them, a glass of wine in his hand now.

"Well?" he demanded. "Did you find these 'bushwhackers' you were looking for?"

"You know we didn't," Longarm snapped. "You've probably got 'em hid away somewhere. This is a big place; who knows how many rooms you've got where you could stash a couple of men?"

"I swear to you I had nothing to do with the attempt on your life." Ortiz smiled, turning his mouth into an ugly slash across his face. "I would not cheat myself of the very satisfying vengeance I will have when my curse does its work, gringo."

Longarm started to step toward the *brujo*, but Packer stopped him with a hand on his arm. "That's enough," the sheriff said. "We looked around the place like you wanted, Marshal, and you got to admit we didn't find nothin'. I think we'd best leave now."

"Leave?" repeated Longarm. "You know as well as I do that Ortiz was behind that ambush!"

"Knowin' somethin' and provin' it are two different things," Packer said quietly. "Come on, Marshal, don't put me in a bad spot here."

Longarm nodded curtly. "Reckon you're right, Sheriff. I just tend to lose my temper when somebody tries to part my hair with a bullet."

Ortiz laughed and said, "Your fate will not be so simple, gringo."

Packer still had hold of Longarm's arm. He steered Longarm toward the door. Longarm looked back at Ortiz and said, "Don't cross me again, El Pollo. Try it and you'll wind up with your feathers plucked good and proper, curse or no curse."

Glaring murderously, Ortiz watched the two lawmen go. When they were outside again and the wrought-iron gate had slammed shut behind them, Packer heaved a sigh. "Somethin' about that feller makes me feel like somebody's walkin' on my grave. I'm glad to be out o' there."

"You know good and well Ortiz sent those gunmen after me," Longarm complained as he and Packer began walking away from the estate.

"No, sir, I don't. That just ain't Ortiz's style. A gent in his line of work relies a lot on keepin' folks scared of him. If people don't believe in his powers, then he ain't nothin'. If you was found shot dead, it wouldn't do a thing to convince folks that Ortiz was responsible. Like he said, he's got somethin' else in mind for you. So I'd sure keep my eyes open, was I you."

"I plan on it," Longarm said, then added, "And what you say makes a lot of sense, Sheriff. If Ortiz wasn't behind that bushwhacking, though, then who was?"

"Man like you's bound to have made a few enemies in his time," Packer pointed out. "You leave any of 'em alive behind you?"

"A few," Longarm admitted. "I suppose somebody who has a grudge against me could've wound up in Rockport and seen me get off the stage earlier today, or even spotted me later. I haven't been hiding." He shook his head. "It's not going to make it easy, knowing I've got to conduct an investigation and watch out not only for Ortiz but for somebody else who wants to see me dead."

"Well," Packer said, "nobody ever claimed upholdin' the law was easy, did they?"

"Nope," Longarm said. "They surely didn't."

Chapter 6

Nobody else tried to bushwhack Longarm, but the evening's events had made him edgy enough so that he didn't sleep particularly well. He tossed and turned for a while, then finally dozed off sometime after midnight. By daylight, he was up and eating sausage and biscuits and gravy at a nearby hash house, since the Rockport House's dining room wasn't open yet. The food was plain but good, and so was the coffee he used to wash it down.

When he was finished, he walked down the street to the first livery stable he came to and rented a fair-looking chestnut gelding. "Ain't much of a cow pony," the elderly hostler told him while saddling the horse, "but easy to handle and it'll go all day."

"Just what I need," Longarm told him, handing over some of the Justice Department's expense money.

From the livery stable he swung by Sheriff Packer's office and left the chestnut tied up at the rack outside. Packer was sitting at his desk as Longarm came in. The local lawman glanced up and asked, "Ain't nobody else tried to shoot you since last night, I hope?"

Longarm shook his head. "Nope. I'm fixing to ride up the coast a ways and take a look at the places where those dead sailors were found. You happen to have a map of the area?"

Packer stood up and gestured toward the wall behind him, where Longarm had already spotted a survey map of the coastal bend. As Longarm came around to stand beside him, the sheriff put a finger on the map and said, "Here's Rockport. Easiest way to get where you're goin' is ride up through Fulton. There's a ferry a couple of miles beyond there that'll take you across Copano Bay, unless you want to ride way the hell and gone around where the bay comes inland. That'll be twenty miles or more out of your way, though."

"I don't mind taking a ferry," Longarm told him.

"All right, once you get to the other side, Copano Bay's to the west, St. Charles Bay to the east. You'll see a road that leads on down to St. Charles Bay. Take it, turn north when you get to the bay, and after you've gone about two miles you'll be where one of the bodies was found. The other one was about half a mile farther on." Packer traced the route on the map with his finger as he gave Longarm the directions.

Longarm nodded, committing the geography of the area to memory. He asked, "Is there anything else you've thought of about those killings that might help me?"

"Nary a thing," Packer replied as he shook his grizzled head. "It's a plumb mystery to me."

"Well, I'll see if I can get to the bottom of it." Longarm lifted a hand in farewell and left the sheriff's office.

It was a pretty morning. The sticky heat that would build up later in the day hadn't begun to develop yet, and the wind blowing in from the gulf was fresh and cool. A few white clouds drifted overhead in the pale blue sky. Longarm followed the road Packer had indicated on the map, which led him along the shore right beside the gulf. He knew there was a barrier island a few miles out there across the water, but he couldn't see it from where he was. As far as he was concerned, those waves washing up on the beach might have been rolling in all the way from Yucatan.

The chestnut proved to be an easy-gaited mount. Longarm rocked gently in the saddle, which was a western-style rig rather than the McClellan which he often used. As he rode, he undid the string tie from around his neck, stuffed it in his pocket, opened his collar, and rolled up the sleeves of his shirt. It promised to be a long day, and he might as well get comfortable, he reasoned.

The road along the shore ran in front of several substantial-looking houses, two- and three-story structures behind broad green lawns. There were also quite a few smaller dwellings, neat little cottages a lot like the one where Blanca lived. Occasionally, piers jutted out into the water on the other side of the road, and Longarm saw quite a few people fishing, leaning on the pier railings with cane poles in their hands and lines dangling in the water. A man could do worse than retire to a place like this, Longarm thought—if he was anywhere near retiring age, which he certainly wasn't. Given his line of work, it was entirely likely he would never reach that age either. But he would keep this place in mind if he did.

At the moment, he had work to do, and he kept the chestnut moving at a good pace as he rode through the mostly residential community of Fulton and then reached the ferry landing at the mouth of Copano Bay. The water stretched for about a mile across the gap. A small steam ferryboat was chugging slowly toward the landing where Longarm waited.

He bought a ticket from a gnarled old-timer who sat in the shade of a little shack beside the landing. "You a stranger around here, mister?" the old man asked.

"Sure am." Longarm grinned. "You look like you're not."

As he had suspected, the old-timer was just looking for an excuse to talk. "Been sailin' up and down this here coast, man and boy, for nigh on to sixty years. There ain't many coves I ain't fished."

"Then you were in these parts when the Kronks were around before."

The old man snorted. "I seen 'em, all right. The men weren't so bad. Big, tall fellas, they were, bigger'n most Injuns. The women was uglier'n pig shit, though. And o' course they was all nasty critters. Cannibals, you know."

"I hear tell they've maybe come back. I'm a mite worried about riding around here."

"You ain't got nothin' to worry about. Them Kronks are long gone. If you're talkin' about them two boys who got theirselves killed not long ago, I reckon that didn't have nothin' to do with Kronks. Probably they just got to sparkin' somebody else's wife or sweetie. You know how us sailors are." The old man cackled. "We got all our brains in our pants sometimes."

Longarm grinned and continued to pass the time of day with the old man until the ferry arrived at the landing a few minutes later. He didn't learn anything useful from the conversation, but he considered the time well spent anyway. You never knew when you'd turn up something important by indulging some old geezer's appetite for talk.

The ferry took a good ten minutes to cross the mouth of the bay, and even though Longarm was the only passenger on this trip, the operator, a young man with bushy hair, was evidently in no mood to talk. He stood in the small cabin at the rear of the ferry and ignored Longarm's attempts to strike up a conversation. Maybe he was just concentrating on the business at hand, Longarm thought, and considering that he himself was a gent who had never been particularly comfortable on boats, that might not be such a bad thing.

When the ferry reached the other landing, Longarm led the chestnut off and swung up into the saddle. This peninsula might be surrounded on three sides by water, but Longarm couldn't tell that from where he sat. The finger of land was broad enough so that he couldn't see the bays on either side, only the water that was behind him. He rode a couple of hundred yards and found the road turning off to the southeast that Packer had mentioned. Crudely printed signs told him that the trail straight ahead led to the town of Tivoli, while the road branching off to the right would take him to St. Charles Bay. He took that road and urged the horse into a trot.

The landscape here was completely flat, as flat as any desert Longarm had ever seen. It was thickly wooded in places, although none of the trees were overly tall, and in other places saw grass waved in the breeze. In the wooded areas the underbrush was often so thick as to be almost impenetrable. Longarm was grateful for the road he was following. It twisted and turned to avoid some sloughs and led past just about the biggest damned live oak Longarm had ever seen. The trunk of the tree was enormous, and its branches spread out in a canopy wide enough to shade a small army, it seemed like. Only a few hundred yards past the big tree, Longarm came to St. Charles Bay.

There was a trail leading alongside the bay, just as Packer had told him. As he rode along the path, he watched the shoreline some fifty yards to his right, just beyond a narrow strip of saw grass. The bay was narrow enough so that he could see either an island or another peninsula on the far side of the water. As he rode along, several large, ungainly birds were startled by his presence and launched into the air from where they had been perched on the limbs of scrubby trees near the water. There were plenty of seagulls in this part of the country, but these birds were some sort of crane, Longarm judged. They looked a lot more graceful in the air than they did on the ground.

This was a peaceful-looking place, thought Longarm. Not at all the kind of scene anybody would associate with murders and cannibal Indians. But he knew from long experience that death could strike just about anywhere and anytime. It was his job to find out how and why these particular deaths had occurred.

There was nothing to indicate exactly where the bodies had been found. From what Sheriff Packer had told him, Longarm could estimate where the sites were, but as far as he could see, locating the precise spots didn't matter. All the shore along here was basically the same—a narrow sand beach bordered by saw grass that was dotted with an occasional clump of brush and trees. There was nothing to indicate why two men had been killed here and their hearts evidently carved out of their bodies and eaten.

Longarm reined in, took a cheroot from his pocket, lit it, blew out a cloud of smoke, and sighed. So far, with the exception of a few annoyances like El Pollo and that blasted curse, this assignment had been fairly pleasant. But now he was running up against an unpleasant reality—the damned case was practically a dead end. The murder victims were unremarkable; just plain sailors from what he had been able to learn. The only thing that made their deaths unusual was the mutilation of the bodies. Longarm was faced with the arduous chore of riding up and down the coast and asking everybody he came across if they had seen or heard anything strange lately, and that could take days or even weeks.

The sound of hoofbeats came suddenly to his ears and made him straighten in the saddle. He hipped around to look behind him and saw half a dozen riders coming toward him. The horsebackers were dressed cowboy, and several of them were carrying Winchesters across their saddles. Longarm pulled the chestnut around so that he would be facing the newcomers as they rode up.

To a man, they looked grim and almost angry. They spread out in a rough half-circle as they came up to Longarm, and since he had the waters of the bay at his back, he was effectively surrounded. He didn't let that spook him, though. He just sat there until the riders had all reined in, then nodded curtly to the gent who had come to a stop directly in front of him. The man eased his horse forward a couple of steps as Longarm said, "Howdy."

"Who the hell are you?" the rider demanded bluntly.

Longarm had been prepared to bring out his badge and identify himself, but the cowboy's attitude rubbed him the wrong way. Instead, he said, "I reckon I could ask the same of you fellas."

"We belong here. You don't."

"How do you know that?" asked Longarm.

One of the other riders spoke up. " 'Cause you don't ride for the Circle H and we do. Harry asked you a question. You'd damn well better answer him."

Longarm looked from face to face and saw that all of them were hostile. The men who weren't carrying rifles had their hands on the butts of their pistols. He had seen enough angry rannies in his time to know that if he didn't handle this carefully, they might decide to string him up from one of the thick limbs of that massive live oak.

"Didn't know this was part of the Circle H spread," Longarm said mildly. "If I'm trespassing, I'll leave."

"This is Haywood land, all right," the first cowboy who had spoken told him. "All the way up to Tivoli and inland nearly to Cardwell. We don't like strangers traipsin' across it, neither."

Longarm shrugged. "I thought this was a public road."

"It is, but the rest ain't."

"No crime in riding on a public road," Longarm pointed out. He didn't want to get these punchers too riled up, but damned if he was going to let them buffalo him, either.

One of the cowboys leaned over and spat disgustedly. "I say we run him the hell off, Harry," he declared, "and if he don't want to go . . . well, we all got ropes."

"Now just hold on, mister," Longarm began as several of the punchers started edging their horses toward him. He didn't want to get into a shooting scrape with these men, because with six-to-one odds, any corpse-and-cartridge session was likely to wind up with him as the corpse. He started to lift a hand toward his vest, hoping to get the folder containing his badge and identification papers out of his pocket before any real trouble started.

A gun blasted abruptly, but the shot didn't come from any of the riders surrounding Longarm. They jerked around in their saddles as a shout followed on the heels of the gun blast. "Hold on!" a woman's voice called. "Hold on there, damn it!"

Longarm saw another rider galloping toward them at breakneck speed, trailed by two more horsebackers. The rider in the lead, the one who had touched off that shot and then hollered at the cowboys to stop, had long blond hair that was whipped behind her by the wind as she rode speedily toward them. She wore boots and jeans and rode astraddle, and even at a distance Longarm could see a good-sized bosom filling out the man's shirt she wore. A broad-brimmed hat dangled from its chin strap and bounced against her back as she urged more speed out of the big black stallion underneath her.

The two men riding behind the young woman looked to be typical cowhands, just like the group that had braced Longarm. The woman was anything but typical, however, Longarm saw as she brought her mount to a skidding stop. Not only did she ride like a veteran of a dozen trail drives, but she had a shell belt strapped around her hips and a man-sized Colt .45 in her hand, which she didn't holster as she faced Longarm.

"Who are you, mister, and what are you doing here?" she demanded.

"That's what these gents wanted to know," Longarm replied as he nodded toward the six cowboys. "They weren't too polite about it either. Don't tell me, ma'am, that you ride for the Circle H too?"

"My father owns it," she told him curtly as she pushed back a strand of blond hair that had fallen in her face as she reined in. "I'm Billie Haywood."

"Custis Long—as I was about to tell these punchers, Deputy United States Marshal Custis Long."

Billie Haywood's eyes widened in surprise. The cowboy called Harry asked sharply, "You're a lawman? Why in blazes didn't you say so?"

"You fellas were too proddy to let me get around to it," Longarm said, his voice cool.

Harry's tone was sullen as he said, "Yeah, well, we've had some trouble around here lately. You can't blame us for bein' a mite suspicious."

"You mean those dead bodies that were found along here?" Longarm asked.

Billie Haywood said, "That . . . and some other things. But on behalf of the Circle H, Marshal, I apologize. You *can* prove you're who you say you are, can't you?"

Longarm took out the leather folder and handed it to her as she moved her horse up next to the rented chestnut. She studied the badge and the papers for a moment before handing them back.

"Reckon you're the genuine article, all right," she said. "Are you here to investigate those killings, Marshal?"

"That . . . and some other things," Longarm said, returning the same cryptic answer she had given him. "Now that you've called off these gents, you think I could ask you a few questions?"

"You can do that while I'm taking you back to the house," Billie Haywood told him. She turned to the punchers who had accosted Longarm. "You boys go on about your work. You know how the cattle like to wander into those sloughs and bog down if we don't watch 'em."

Grudgingly, Harry touched a finger to the brim of his hat and said, "Yeah, sure, Miss Billie." He jerked his head at the other men. "Come on."

They turned and rode off, leaving behind the two men who had accompanied Billie as she interrupted the standoff between Longarm and the other Circle H riders. She inclined her head toward them and told Longarm, "They sort of keep an eye on me these days, what with all the strange doings hereabouts. My dad's idea."

"And a good one, too, I'd say," Longarm commented. "What's this about taking me to the house?"

"You're coming back to ranch headquarters with me. I want my father to meet you, and if you're going to be poking around on his spread, it's the least you can do."

Longarm nodded. Chances were he would have gotten around to talking to the owner of this land anyway.

He and Billie Haywood fell in alongside each other as they rode. The two punchers who served as Billie's bodyguards trailed along behind. Longarm commented, "That fella Harry and his pards were mighty touchy. Acted like they thought I was a cow thief or something."

"Cows aren't what we've been losing," Billie said.

Longarm glanced over at her, wondering what in blazes she meant by that. From the tight set of her face, though, she wasn't in any mood to answer. Still, it wouldn't hurt to ask. "Having some other sort of trouble, are you?"

"Now that I've thought about it, you ought to wait and ask your questions of my father. This is his ranch, and it's not my place to talk too much."

Longarm didn't agree with that, but he didn't want to spend all his time arguing with this young woman. He could tell from the firm line of her jaw that she could be as stubborn as an old mule if she wanted to. He muttered, "All right, I'll talk to your pa."

It took about twenty minutes of steady riding to reach the headquarters of the Circle H. The house sat beside the water, facing the bay from behind a large stretch of open ground. Longarm managed not to let out a whistle of surprise as he took in the sight of the huge, sprawling house. It was practically a mansion, with three stories and a lot of Victorian-looking architecture. There were more than enough spires and cupolas and tall narrow windows to go around. A weather vane stood atop the tallest point of the house and was spinning merrily in the offshore breeze.

Behind the house were several outbuildings, including a barn, some corrals, and a bunkhouse. A long dock jutted out into the bay in front of the house. There was a tall boathouse attached to the pier, and a small sailboat sat tied to the end of the dock. All in all, the place was a curious mixture of elements from both the range and the sea. This was cattle country, true, but around here nobody could get away from the influence of the ocean for very long.

Billie reined in and dismounted, and Longarm followed suit. She handed the black stallion's reins to one of the cowboys and motioned for Longarm to do the same. "Come inside," she told him. "I'll introduce you to Dad."

He went with her along a flagstone walk and up several steep steps to a porch of polished hardwood. Longarm wasn't sure how they kept the boards so shiny in this salt air. Probably had somebody whose job was just to polish them every day, he decided. The front door was a heavy, ornately carved mahogany affair with a huge brass doorknob, but despite the door's massiveness, it swung open easily under Billie's touch. Maybe when the fella was through polishing the porch, he spent a few minutes each day oiling those hinges, Longarm thought. Billie took him into a foyer with a parquet floor and velvet on the walls. Longarm refrained from mentioning that it looked a little like the entrance to a fancy whorehouse.

She took his arm and tugged him through an arched entrance into a parlor that was dominated by a huge stone hearth. "We have steam heat throughout the whole house," she said, "but nothing beats a fire when the weather's cold and raw."

"Yes, ma'am," Longarm said. He didn't add that a fireplace was mighty nice for cozying up in front of with a pretty girl, a description that fit Billie just fine.

She let go of his arm, put her hands on her hips, and turned around, giving him a good view of the firm but rounded rump filling the seat of those denim trousers below the slanting line of her gunbelt. She called, "Dad? Are you here? I've brought a visitor."

Longarm looked around the room while they were waiting for a response. This looked more like the parlor of a ranch house in cow country. An impressive set of long horns hung over the hearth, and a tall, glass-fronted cabinet filled with rifles and shotguns was tucked in one corner. A hooked rug was on the floor. The furniture consisted of a sofa and several chairs that were overstuffed and sturdily built. The only concession to a feminine touch was another glass-fronted cabinet, this one occupied by an array of tiny figurines carved out of glass, crystal, pewter, and ceramics. The ornaments were incredibly detailed, he saw as he took off his hat and leaned closer to the cabinet to study them, and he wondered who had amassed the collection. Somehow, it didn't seem like the sort of thing a young woman like Billie would do.

"Those were my mother's," she said as if reading his mind. "My father likes to keep them here to remind him of her."

"She's passed on, I reckon?"

Billie nodded. "When I was just a little girl. I only barely remember her. Frank recalls her better than I do."

"Frank?"

"My brother," Billie said.

Before she could go on, a door on the other side of the room opened and a man rolled through it, sitting in a chair with big wooden wheels on the sides. He had probably been quite powerful at some point in his life, but time and illness had wasted him away until his clothes hung on him loosely. His legs didn't move at all. He propelled himself into the room by using his arms and hands to turn the wheels of the chair. Those arms and his shoulders were the only things still big about him.

Despite his crippled state, fire flashed in his eyes as he studied the visitor in his parlor. "Good morning to you, sir," he said while rolling himself forward. He lifted his right hand and extended it toward Longarm. "I'm Jesse Haywood. Welcome to my home."

"Custis Long, sir," Longarm introduced himself. He took Haywood's hand, and found the rancher's grip to be every bit as powerful as he expected.

"Harry and some of the boys had Marshal Long cornered over by the bay," Billie put in. "I saw them while I was out riding and figured something was going on, so I rode over to put a stop to it. Sure enough, the boys were making noises about stringing folks up."

Haywood frowned. "Did my daughter say *Marshal* Long, sir?"

"Deputy U.S. marshal out of Denver," Longarm explained. "I'm down here looking into the murders of those two sailors who were found on what I reckon must be your land."

"Indeed it is," Haywood said with a curt nod. "Has been ever since my father claimed it after fighting alongside old Sam Houston in the revolution back in '36. The Haywood ranch was one of the first cattle spreads in the coastal bend." Pride filled the old man's voice. "I was a youngster then, a sprout of ten years old, but I remember it quite clearly."

Longarm nodded, doing some quick ciphering and figuring that Haywood was less than fifty-five years old. His snow-white hair and beard and seamed face made him appear older. The illness that had robbed him of the use of his legs had obviously taken quite a toll on him.

"What do you think of the stories going round about how the Karankawas have come back?" Longarm asked bluntly. "That's one of the possibilities I'm investigating."

Haywood shrugged his shoulders and said, "Billie, there's a pitcher of cold lemonade out in the kitchen. Fetch a glass for Mr. Long and myself." He looked at Longarm. "I'd offer you some coffee or a drink, but that blasted sawbones down in Corpus won't let me keep either one in the house. Says they're bad for me. I don't think that damned pill-pusher knows what he's talking about."

"Lemonade's fine by me," Longarm said. It was getting closer to noon now, and the morning was growing warmer.

"Well, it's not fine as far as I'm concerned," Billie said as she crossed her arms. "I want to stay here while you tell Marshal Long about the Kronks."

Haywood waved a big, knobby-knuckled hand. "A girl-child doesn't need to be hearing stories about a bunch of bloody savages," he told her.

"I'm not a girl-child," she shot back. "I'm a woman, damn it, and I hate the way you try to protect me from the world, Dad."

"Don't know where she got that spiteful mouth," Haywood grumbled, but Longarm could tell the old man didn't really mind Billie defying him. The young woman's obviously stubborn nature was probably another point of pride as far as the rancher was concerned.

"All right," Haywood said, "I'll tell you what I think, Marshal. From what I've heard, it sounds like those killings could have been done by a band of Kronks. Why they came back and where they came back from, I couldn't tell you, but the details of those murders sure match up with the stories I heard about the Karankawas while I was growing up."

"How come nobody's seen 'em?" Longarm asked.

"They were always as much at home on the water as on land," Haywood replied. "They traveled up and down the coast by canoe and knew all the little bays and inlets. They could be hiding out over on San Jose Island or up on Matagorda. Nothing much over there but sand dunes and saw grass, but that'd be enough for those savages and nobody would bother them there."

Longarm groaned inwardly. If he had to search the two long barrier islands Haywood had mentioned, that would mean another boat trip and one hell of a lot of riding once he was over there. The pleasant aspects of this job were rapidly vanishing.

"I think the Kronks are back too," Billie said. "When they ate their victims, Dad, did they eat the private parts too?"

"Billie!" Haywood roared, finally pushed too far by his daughter. "That ain't a proper question for a young lady to ask. Now get out there in the kitchen and fetch that lemonade!"

She went, but not before flinging an impudent glance toward Longarm. He wasn't sure what to make of Miss Billie Haywood, but he was willing to bet that even an able-bodied man would have had his hands full raising her.

"You'll have to forgive Billie, Marshal Long," Haywood went on. "I'm afraid to my everlasting vexation that I taught the girl to speak her mind."

"Doesn't bother me any, Mr. Haywood. I like a woman who ain't afraid to speak up. But right now I'm more concerned about the job that brought me here. Miss Billie hinted that something else a mite unusual has been going on around here. Besides those two killings, I mean."

Again the rancher shrugged his still-broad shoulders. "We've had a few riders disappear," he said.

Longarm's brow furrowed in a frown. "Disappear?" he repeated.

"It's not like their horses came back with bloody saddles or anything. But several times the hands have gotten up in the morning and found somebody missing from the bunkhouse. Their gear would still be there, but they'd be gone. No sign of trouble anywhere, and nobody heard anything unusual during the night."

"Did you report this to Sheriff Packer over in Rockport?" Longarm asked, his frown deepening.

"What was there to report? The men who disappeared had been riding horses from my remuda, didn't have mounts of their own. The gear they left behind wasn't worth much of anything, either. None of 'em stole anything when they left. I figure they just got tired of riding for the Circle H and walked off. There's a stagecoach runs between Lamar and Tivoli; they could've caught one of those coaches easy enough and from Tivoli gone on to just about anywhere they wanted."

"Without drawing their pay?"

"Well, as it happens none of them had much pay coming. They disappeared less than a week after payday each time." Haywood clasped his hands together and leaned forward. "Oh, it's strange, I'll warrant that. But it didn't seem like a matter for the law, and you've got to admit, Marshal, there's no way it could be connected with whoever killed those poor sailors."

"Don't see how it could be," Longarm muttered as much to himself as to Haywood.

"The rest of the hands are on edge about it, though, like a trail herd that doesn't want to settle down because there's a storm on the horizon. They're just waiting for a good reason to stampede. This business about the Kronks coming back doesn't help matters any."

Longarm had punched enough cattle in his earlier days to know exactly what Haywood was talking about. The whole gulf coast seemed a mite skittish these days, and maybe with good reason.

Billie returned with a tray containing a pitcher of lemonade and two glasses. Longarm smiled at her as she poured for him and her father. Then, as she handed him the glass he asked her, "You're not having any?"

"Heavens, no!" she exclaimed in mock surprise. "Why, this lemonade might be too strong for a mere girl-child like me."

"Billie . . ." Haywood said warningly.

"I'll leave you two gentlemen alone," she went on demurely. Haywood just stared after her in exasperation as she left the parlor and shut the door behind her.

"You'd never know it," the old rancher said, "but she's a mighty pretty filly when she wants to be, and just as sweet as molasses, too."

"I can believe that," Longarm said as he sipped the lemonade. It was cold and good. He didn't say anything else, but even though he had only known Billie Haywood for a short time, he sort of had the feeling he preferred her just the way she had been so far—intelligent, opinionated, and damned attractive.

Chapter 7

At Jesse Haywood's insistence, Longarm stayed at the ranch house for lunch, and he was glad he did. The Mexican cook and housekeeper had prepared fried chicken, mashed potatoes, greens, and peach cobbler. All of it made a fine meal, washed down with more of the lemonade.

There was an empty chair at the table, however, and Longarm, recalling that Billie had mentioned having a brother, asked about him.

"Frank?" Billie said with a snort before her father could reply to Longarm's question. "He's up in the attic."

Longarm frowned.

"He's too busy with those observations of his to bother coming down and having a meal like somebody normal," Billie went on.

A new voice said, "I heard that!"

Longarm turned his head and saw a young man, maybe three or four years older than Billie, coming into the spacious dining room. He wore a brown suit and a white shirt, the clothes so wrinkled he might have slept in them for a week. A pair of spectacles were perched on his nose, and his thick dark hair was rumpled. He combed his fingers through it as he came up to the table.

"Hello, who's this?" the young man asked as he looked at Longarm.

"Deputy Marshal Long," Haywood said. "He's looking into those killings that everybody's blaming on the Kronks. Marshal, this is my son Frank."

Longarm stood up and extended a hand to Frank Haywood. "Glad to meet you, Frank," he said. "I've been visiting with your father and your sister."

"Kronks," Frank said as he shook Longarm's hand. "I don't recall . . . Oh, yes, those Indians who were rumored to be cannibals. I recall Father mentioning them when I was younger."

Longarm sat down again, and Frank settled into the empty chair across the table. "What do you think about this business, Frank?" Longarm asked.

"About the murders?" The young man shook his head. "I'm afraid I haven't given it much thought at all. I've been quite busy lately."

"With his observations," Billie said dryly.

Frank leaned forward, ignoring the plate of food the housekeeper placed in front of him, and regarded Longarm intently. He said, "There's a barometrical occlusion developing, you know."

"No," Longarm said slowly, "I didn't know that."

"Well, there is. There's going to be a storm soon, perhaps even a hurricane as strong as the one that struck Indianola a few years ago. I predicted that hurricane, of course. If I had only been able to pinpoint its location better, I might have been able to save some of the people who lost their lives. But it was impossible to know precisely where the storm was going to come ashore." Frank sighed. "Just as I don't know exactly where or when this new storm will strike. But it's out there in the gulf, I can assure you of that."

"You're talking about predicting the weather," Longarm said.

"Of course. What else would my observations be for?"

69

Longarm nodded, understanding now what Frank was getting at. "You study the signs, like seeing which way the birds perch on a tree limb or counting the hairs on a wooly-worm."

Frank Haywood looked aghast at the suggestion. "Really, Marshal Long! My observations are strictly grounded in the scientific method. I study the patterns of temperature and wind variation, as well as the barometrical forces. I've kept a running log of my predictions, and they've proven to be accurate over half the time."

"Is that so? I knew an old man who could tell when it was going to rain because the joints got to hurting in his right leg, which he didn't have anymore because it got blown off by a cannonball during the Mexican War. But the pains were still there, and he could sure tell when it was going to come a gully-washer."

Frank looked dubious as he said, "I know that some people put their faith in such beliefs, but the science of weather prognostication—"

"Oh, shut up and prognosticate your lunch, why don't you?" Billie burst out. "Don't encourage him, Marshal. Dad and I have to listen to this all the time."

Frank looked injured but fell silent, and Longarm felt a little sorry for him. He imagined Frank had to put up with quite a bit from Billie's sharp tongue. None of which was any of his business, of course, but he sort of liked the young man, even if Frank did get a mite tedious about his hobby. Frank started in on a couple more occasions during the meal, but Billie shut him up both times.

When lunch was over, Frank asked, "While you're here, would you like to see my observation post, Marshal?"

Longarm started to refuse as graciously as he could, then remembered what Billie had said about Frank being up in the attic. Suddenly it seemed to him like a good idea to take a look around the area, something that was difficult to do where there wasn't any high ground. The attic of the Haywood house might be the next-best thing.

"Sure, I'd like that, Frank," he said, ignoring the way Billie rolled her eyes.

Frank led Longarm upstairs to the third floor by way of the usual staircases, then took him down a hall to a door that opened onto a spiral staircase. Frank climbed the stairs first, his footsteps echoing hollowly as Longarm followed him. The shaft through which the staircase ran was dark and gloomy.

It opened into a bright, airy room, however, and Longarm realized the chamber was at the top of one of the house's towers. Large windows on all four sides were raised to let in the ocean breezes. From here there was a good view of the weathervane at the other end of the house. A low, benchlike table ran all the way around the walls of the room, and it was filled with open journals and instruments the likes of which Longarm had never seen.

"That's a quicksilver barometer," Frank said, pointing to an apparatus that included a tall glass tube partially filled with the liquid metal. "I have a temperature gauge over here, and a wind-speed indicator that I constructed, and a rain gauge—"

"Mighty impressive," Longarm said, cutting in before Frank could run through the entire list of his weather-predicting equipment. "You can see a mighty long way from up here, can't you?"

"Of course. The more information about weather conditions that I can gather, the more accurately I can predict what will happen."

A man could certainly see a far piece, as the old-timers said, Longarm thought. The coastal plain spread out to the west and northwest, turning into the brush country of the Nueces Strip farther inland, while to the east and southeast were water, marshlands, water, live oak thickets, water, sand dunes, and more water. From up here, Longarm could see Copano Bay, St. Charles Bay, several peninsulas, and San Jose Island. Miles to the southwest he could pick out the roofs of buildings in Fulton and Rockport. And that was just with the naked eye. If a man had a good spyglass—like the one Longarm had just noted on Frank Haywood's workbench—he could keep track

71

of just about all the comings and goings in this part of the country.

"Frank," Longarm said solemnly, "I got a proposition for you. More of a favor, actually."

"Concerning the case that brought you here, Marshal?"

"That's right."

"I'd be glad to do anything I can to help, of course," the young man said, "but I'm afraid I don't know anything about investigating a crime. My interests tend more to the scientific."

"All I want you to do is keep an eye out and let me know if you see anything funny going on around here," Longarm explained. "Anything at all that seems out of the ordinary. Can you do that?"

"I suppose so." Frank grinned suddenly. "This is what they call keeping a weather eye out, isn't it? I'm certainly suited for that, and well situated, too."

"That's what I thought. I'm staying at the Rockport House. You can get in touch with me there or at least leave a message for me if you run across anything you think I ought to know about."

"I'll be pleased to do that, Marshal."

"Wish I could tell you there'll be some compensation involved if this pans out, but I can't promise that. The government gets mighty tightfisted sometimes. . . ."

Frank waved off the offer. "Don't worry about that. I'm up here most of the time anyway, just looking around. I might as well put my observations to some practical use."

"Well, if you could figure out how to know far enough ahead of time when bad weather was going to hit, that'd be downright practical," Longarm observed. "And mighty helpful sometimes, too."

"I'll keep working on it," Frank promised.

Longarm left the young man in his aerie and went downstairs to say good-bye to Jesse Haywood and Billie. "I'll pass the word to the hands that they're not supposed to bother you if they run into you on the Circle H again," Billie offered.

"I'd appreciate that." Longarm shook hands with Haywood again, then walked out onto the porch with Billie following him.

"*Are* you going to be back this way again?" she persisted.

Longarm shrugged. "A man in my business never knows where his work's going to take him. How come you want to know?"

"I can't be spending all my time gallivanting around the ranch looking out for you," she snapped. "Somebody's got to look after things, what with Dad the way he is—and Frank the way *he* is."

Longarm thought there was a bit of a blush coloring her cheeks, and if anything it made her even prettier. He tried not to grin too broadly as he said, "I'd say there's a good chance I'll be back. Even if I clear up this case, I'll try to stop by and let you know how it turned out."

"If you get a chance," Billie said casually, but Longarm suspicioned she wasn't feeling casual at all.

He let things go at that and mounted the rented chestnut, swinging the horse back toward the ferry landing. The route he took was a little more direct this time. Since studying the terrain hereabouts from Frank Haywood's crow's nest, he had a pretty good idea how to get back to the landing without having to follow the trail that hugged the shoreline of the bay. He cut cross-country instead, and as he rode he thought about what he had discovered so far today.

It wasn't a whole hell of a lot. The old man at the ferry had scoffed at the idea of the Kronks coming back, while Jesse Haywood had seemed to think it was possible. The scenes of the murders hadn't told him anything. There was the business about some of the Circle H riders disappearing, but Longarm was damned if he could see how that had anything to do with anything else. His next move was just as deep a mystery to him.

Abruptly, he reined in as he noticed something he hadn't seen before. Nestled in one of those groves of oak trees was a small stone building, and beyond it was a cleared, cultivated

73

area. Several men in baggy white shirts and trousers and a few women in long skirts were working in the field, hoeing and weeding and planting. For a moment, Longarm wondered what a garden like that was doing right in the middle of a cattle spread. Maybe the Circle H grew fresh vegetables for the crew there, using Mexican laborers to tend the garden. Then Longarm spotted the small white cross on top of the stone building, and his puzzlement grew.

He heeled the horse into a trot that carried him over to the building. As he rode up, a man in a long brown robe appeared in the open doorway. The priest was a slender man with fine features and gray hair, and he lifted a hand in greeting as Longarm reined in.

"Good day to you, sir," the priest said. "Can I help you?"

"Howdy, Padre. I was just visiting the Haywoods, and I noticed this place over here on my way back to the ferry landing. Didn't know there was a mission around here."

"Yes, this is the Mission San Ignacio." The priest smiled. "It's been here for many years, and Mr. Haywood has been kind enough to allow us to continue using it, even though the land is now part of his ranch."

Longarm leaned forward in the saddle, easing muscles that started to cramp up if he sat still for too long. He said, "I reckon the Spaniards must've built this place, from the looks of it. Mighty ancient."

The priest nodded. "It was built in 1682. There are church records concerning its construction in the archives in Rome. Ever since that time, it has served the poor people of this area, such as those currently laboring in our gardens." He waved a hand toward the workers. "Would you like to get down and have some cool water, my friend? I'm afraid we have little else to offer you."

Longarm shook his head and said, "No, that's all right, Padre. I've got to be riding on, but I wanted to stop and find out if you might've seen anything unusual going on around here lately. You see, I'm a deputy U.S. marshal, and I'm looking into those killings over by the bay."

The priest's friendly expression disappeared. "You've come to persecute people who couldn't have had anything to do with those crimes?" he asked.

"Not hardly," Longarm exclaimed, surprised by the man's vehemence. "All I'm interested in is the truth. You don't think the Kronks could've done those killings?"

"Of course not. There haven't been any Karankawas in this area for many, many years. I've heard the rumors going around, and they're ridiculous."

"Could be you're right," Longarm allowed. "If that's the case, that's fine with me. All I really want is to find out who killed those sailor boys. By the way, my name's Custis Long."

"I'm Father Terence."

"Thought I heard an Irish accent," Longarm said, hoping to put the man at ease again. "You've been over here a good while, but originally you're a son of the auld sod, right?"

"I was born in Ireland, yes," Father Terence said with a nod. He seemed to relax a little as he continued. "I'm sorry I almost lost my temper, Marshal Long. I just hate to hear all these unfounded rumors going around. The Lord has little patience for gossip."

"Maybe not, but in my business it can sometimes come in handy," Longarm pointed out. "If you hear anything that might help me, Padre, I'm staying at the Rockport House, over across the bay. I'd appreciate it if you'd let me know."

"Of course. It was a pleasure meeting you, Marshal. *Vaya con Dios.*"

Longarm gave the priest a friendly nod and rode on, heading for the ferry landing. He didn't expect Father Terence to come up with any information that would help him, but you never knew about things like that. The one fact that was sometimes necessary to break a case wide open could come from just about anywhere, Longarm had discovered in his years of toting a federal badge.

As he had thought, the route he took to the landing turned out to be shorter—not that it really mattered, since he had to wait quite a while for the ferry to arrive once he got there. The bushy-haired young man operating the steam engine wasn't any more talkative on the way back across Copano Bay. Longarm at least had some company on this trip, in the form of a farmer and the man's two sons, who were taking a wagonload of melons into Rockport to sell them. The farmer and his boys were all armed, the farmer with a shotgun and the younger men with rifles.

"Can't take no chances these days," the farmer explained as he spat tobacco juice into the waters of the bay. "With them Kronks around and goin' on a rampage, a man's got to carry a gun with him, just in case he's jumped by them savages. Wouldn't even be travelin' if it wasn't for the fact them melons got to get to market or start goin' bad on the vines."

"I understand," Longarm said with a nod. He didn't identify himself as he asked, "You ever actually *seen* any of those Kronks?"

"No, and I don't want to. Figure if I did, it'd be the last thing I'd ever see, 'cause them devils'd be fixin' to rip my heart out." The farmer shook his head. "No, sir, I don't want to see 'em. But I know they're out there, all the same."

That didn't seem to be an uncommon attitude in these parts, Longarm mused. People who believed in the return of the Karankawas were firmly convinced that the threat was real.

He left the farmer and his sons unloading their wagon from the ferry. The chestnut carried him back along the shore to Rockport, and it was late afternoon by the time he got there. He thought about stopping by the sheriff's office, but he didn't really have anything to report to Packer. He wanted to find out what the local lawman knew about the Haywoods, but that could wait. Instead Longarm rode straight to the Rockport House. The hotel had a carriage house that doubled as a stable, and Longarm left the chestnut there to be unsaddled, rubbed down, and given some grain.

At least that curse business hadn't popped up again today, he was thinking as he entered the lobby of the hotel, but then he stopped short and wondered if he had jinxed himself by letting his mind wander like that. For there was Miss Nora Ridgley standing at the desk talking to the clerk, her skinny figure unmistakable even though she had her back to Longarm.

For a second, something brushed across his brain, its touch feather-light. Before he could even come close to grasping it, however, it was gone, and Longarm didn't have the slightest idea what it might have been. He gave a little shake of his head. He wondered if he could slip past Nora without her noticing him.

She seemed intent on her conversation with the clerk, and that was good. It gave Longarm more of a chance to get upstairs without having to fool with the BIA agent. He took a couple of steps toward the stairs when something that Nora was saying caught his attention.

". . . black dog," she said emphatically. The clerk nodded.

Black dog? Longarm thought to himself. What in blazes was she talking about?

"Thank you," Nora said to the clerk. "I'm sure I can find it." She started to turn away from the desk.

Longarm sat down hurriedly in one of the overstuffed armchairs near him. There was a two-day-old copy of the Corpus Christi *Caller* on a small table next to the chair, so he snatched up the newspaper and spread it open in front of him, muttering oaths to himself that he was forced to resort to a trick so old it had whiskers. He just didn't feel like facing Nora after the frustrating day he'd had, though.

She moved past him with a swish of skirts and a hint of lilac water, evidently so absorbed in what she had learned during her conversation with the clerk that she paid no attention to the man sitting in the armchair. The way things had been going, Longarm was thankful even for small favors like that. Instead of leaving the hotel, Nora went to the stairs and disappeared up them, heading for her room, no doubt. That was another lucky break.

He put the paper aside and went over to the desk. The clerk looked up at him and said, "Oh, hello, Marshal Long. You just missed Miss Ridgley."

"You know the old saying about a miss and a mile," Longarm growled. "I saw the two of you talking. What was that business about a black dog?"

"You were *eavesdropping*, Marshal?"

Longarm's dislike for the clerk grew. "Paying attention is part of my job, mister," he said. "Now, are you going to answer my question or not? Why was Miss Ridgley interested in a dog? She ain't thinking of getting a pup, is she?"

"Not that kind of dog," the clerk answered with a sniff. "The Black Dog is the name of a drinking establishment over by the wharves. It's quite a disreputable place, from what I've heard. I've never been there."

Longarm could easily believe that. If this pasty-faced fella in his fancy swallowtail coat ever set foot inside a waterfront tavern, he likely wouldn't come out in one piece. But that still didn't satisfy Longarm's curiosity.

"How come Miss Ridgley was asking about a place like that?"

The clerk shrugged his narrow shoulders. "I'm certain I wouldn't know. She had heard of it, and she asked me how to find it. I told her. That's all right, isn't it, Marshal?"

"Sure, sure," Longarm said distractedly. The wheels of his brain had begun to turn over again.

A moment later he became aware that the clerk had said something else to him. As he looked at the man, the clerk again asked, "Would you like your key, Marshal?"

"Yeah," Longarm nodded. "I'll need my key, all right."

The clerk handed it over, and Longarm went upstairs. He bounced the key on the palm of his hand as he walked slowly down the hall toward his room. As he passed the door of room seven, Nora Ridgley's room, he paused. There were faint sounds coming from inside the room, as if she was moving around. Getting ready to go out again maybe? Getting ready to pay a visit to a tavern called the Black Dog?

Longarm reached down and silently wrapped his hand around the doorknob. He tried to turn it, but it was locked, which didn't surprise him. Nora had struck him as the type to always lock her door, even when she was in the room. He glanced up and down the hall and saw that it was deserted at the moment except for himself. Feeling more than a little foolish, he bent over enough to peer through the keyhole.

He sure as hell wasn't interested in getting an eyeful of nearly naked female flesh, not when the female in question was Nora Ridgley, but that was what he got anyway. She was changing clothes, and she was down to her scanties at the moment, which were a lot lacier and frillier than Longarm would have expected. He'd had her pegged as the plain and simple type. But he didn't waste any time studying on Nora's underwear. As soon as he saw that she hadn't left her key in the lock on the inside of the door, he straightened and slid his own key into the lock from the outside. Trying to be as quiet as he could, he twisted the key and bent it to the side at the same time.

The metal gave under the force of his muscles. The key snapped off in the lock with a sharp sound. Nora called out, "Who's there? What was that?"

Longarm didn't answer. He slipped the part of the key he still held into his pocket, then turned and headed for the stairs again. It would have been nice to wash up and change shirts in his own room, but where he was going it probably wouldn't matter if he smelled a little like horseflesh and sweat. With that key jammed in the lock, Nora's door wasn't going to be opened for a while, and he was counting on that to give him some time.

He wanted to see what was so all-fired interesting about a place called the Black Dog.

Chapter 8

Longarm didn't have any trouble finding the Black Dog. He didn't even have to ask directions from any of the men on the waterfront. The tavern was directly across the street from a long wharf where several tall-masted ships were riding at anchor, and in the fading light from the setting sun Longarm could make out the sign over the door of the place, complete with a crude painting of a huge, snarling black mastiff.

The building itself was a squat frame structure. The wide, warped, unpainted planks were a washed-out gray color from long exposure to the salt air. Longarm watched the tavern from the doorway of a closed apothecary shop for a few minutes and saw several men in the white duck pants and pullover shirts of sailors entering. Seamen were not the only customers of the Black Dog, however. There was a hitch rack in front of the building just like hundreds of others Longarm had seen in frontier towns, and half a dozen horses were tied up there. From the looks of things, cowboys from the inland ranches patronized the Black Dog too.

There wasn't much more he could learn standing around outside, and it was only a matter of time before Nora Ridgley raised a ruckus and got out of her hotel room. Once she was out, she might follow through on her original plan and come here to the tavern. Longarm intended to do some poking around of his own before that happened. Then when Nora showed up, he could steer her out of the place. A woman like Nora wouldn't be very safe in a waterfront grog shop like the Black Dog.

Longarm walked down the block from his makeshift observation post and pushed through the door of the tavern. Inside it was as dim and smoky as he had expected. A bar ran along the left side of the room. There were booths on the right-hand wall, and the space in the center of the room was cluttered with tables, some of them round, some square. The rear wall had a tiny stage on one side, and a door in the other side that probably led to back rooms where a variety of nefarious activities could be conducted.

A dozen men stood at the bar, being served by a sweating, bald-headed bartender wearing an apron that once might have been white. Twice that many patrons were scattered at the tables, some drinking, some playing cards, and others calling out bawdy comments to the two waitresses who moved among them delivering drinks. Just as the bartender's apron bore some vestiges of its original color, the women still possessed a hint of youth and prettiness—but only a hint. The whole scene was lit by several kerosene lanterns suspended from the ceiling, the chimneys of which were so greasy and grimy that the illumination they cast was faint. All in all, the Black Dog reminded Longarm of dozens of other dives he had been in except for one thing.

That was the black dog on the wall.

A twin to the painting on the sign outside, the dog stood on a wide shelf behind the bar, fur bristling with anger, lips drawn back from bared white teeth in a snarling grimace. It appeared ready to spring down from its perch and rip out the throat of anyone who got too close. It might have, too, if it hadn't been dead.

Longarm's eyes widened at the sight of the dog, and for a second he thought the brute was alive. Then he noticed the rattiness of the fur and the fact that somebody had shot out one of its glass eyes. The dog was stuffed like some sort of big-game trophy. Somebody must have been mighty fond of it, Longarm thought, to have such an ugly creature stuffed and mounted like that.

He weaved through the tables and headed toward the bar. As he had thought, the customers were a mixture of sailors and cowboys, and although each group kept to itself, there didn't seem to be any of the hostility Longarm might have expected from such a volatile blend of occupations.

The big man seated on a stool at the end of the bar might have had something to do with that. It was difficult to tell how tall he was with him seated like that, but he was plenty wide, Longarm saw. His bulk wasn't fat, either, but muscle. He had a thatch of red hair and a bushy beard of the same shade. A bung starter lay on the bar at his elbow, and from the looks of him, he could cave in a man's head without even breaking a sweat. Longarm didn't want to put that to the test.

He found an empty spot at the bar and leaned against the scarred hardwood counter until the bartender came over. The bald-headed man didn't ask any questions, just looked at his newest customer until Longarm said, "You wouldn't have any Maryland rye, would you?"

The bartender shook his head but still didn't say anything.

"Well, then, give me a shot of whiskey, as long as it ain't any of that homemade Who-Hit-John. I've had too much of that stuff that's nothing but rattlesnake squeezin's and panther piss."

Reaching under the counter, the bartender brought out a bottle and held it up for Longarm's inspection. The label was one Longarm recognized—but of course that didn't mean the contents were what had originally come in the bottle. Still, he was willing to take a chance, so he nodded. The bartender uncorked the bottle and splashed some of the amber liquid in a glass that wasn't too smudged. He slid it across to Longarm, who took a sip of the stuff and then tossed it back when it didn't completely blister the skin off his insides. "Not bad," he told the bartender as he placed the empty glass on the bar and rattled a coin onto the hardwood next to it. "You ain't a very talkative sort, are you?"

"That'd be difficult, mate," a deep, booming voice replied, but it didn't come from the bartender. "Jacko's tongue was cut out by Malay pirates when we were sailin' the South China Sea."

Longarm looked over to see that the red-bearded man from the end of the bar had gotten down off his stool and lumbered over. As Longarm suspected, the man was rather short, seeming almost as wide as he was tall. There was a friendly grin on his bearded face, but the expression didn't touch his gray eyes.

"I'm Red Mike," the man went on as he stuck out a massive paw. "I own this place. Haven't seen you in here before, have I?"

With a little trepidation, Longarm let Red Mike's hand swallow his own, but the big man's grip was surprisingly gentle. Some of the biggest men were like that and had no need to demonstrate their obvious strength. Longarm said, "My name's Parker," using his own middle name for an alias. "Just got into town, and I was told the Black Dog was the best place to go for a drink."

"Well, I'm glad someone steered you to us, Mr. Parker. In Rockport on business, are you?"

"Yep," Longarm said. "My own business."

Red Mike gave a rumbling laugh. "I assure you, mate, I didn't mean to pry. In here each man keeps his own counsel and minds his own affairs, and that's the way I intend for it to stay." He gestured to the bartender. "Pour another drink for our new friend Mr. Parker, Jacko."

Longarm didn't for a second believe the jovial front Red Mike was putting up. But he was willing to play along in hopes of finding out some information he could use. Mike would probably know more about what went on around here than anybody else.

After he'd knocked back the second drink, Longarm jerked a thumb at the stuffed dog and asked, "How come that critter's up there like that? I thought when I came in the damned thing was alive."

"That's old Flounder," explained Red Mike. "Sailed the seven seas with me, he did. Got the name because whenever we put into port, he'd go boundin' out into the surf and come back with a flounder in his mouth nearly every time. Mean son of a bitch, and no more brains in his head when he was alive than there is now. My crews always hated him."

"Then why'd you keep him?" Longarm asked.

"Because he had one quality that made him worth every bit of trouble he caused. He was loyal to me. I slept sound in my bunk every night knowin' that no bloody mutineers could come skulkin' around with Flounder there. He'd have torn their throats out if they'd tried to get near me."

Longarm nodded. "I reckon I can see why that'd make you fond of him, all right. Had trouble with your crews, did you?"

Red Mike shrugged his massive shoulders and said, "There's always one or two malcontents in every bunch. If you're lucky, that's all and you can deal with them. Sometimes it's harder. I never had a ship taken away from me, though, you can bet on that."

"I reckon so," Longarm muttered. He couldn't picture anybody trying to rebel against Red Mike's rule and getting away with it. He figured more than one would-be mutineer had wound up swinging from a yardarm on the ships captained by this red-bearded giant.

This was interesting but wasn't getting him anywhere. He went on. "I'm trying to put together a crew myself. Maybe you could give me a hand and recommend some boys who'd be good for the job."

"Aye, I know most of the sailors in this part of the world, Mr. Parker. I'd be glad to put out the word that you're lookin' for a crew, especially if . . ." Red Mike let his voice trail off meaningfully.

Longarm patted his vest pocket. "Don't worry," he said. "I can take care of you, friend, if you take care of me."

"Then I think we'll be doin' some business," said Red Mike with a grin.

Longarm took note of the fact that the tavern owner hadn't asked why he needed a ship's crew. To a man like Red Mike, that probably wouldn't matter. As long as he got his payoff for helping assemble the crew, that was all he would care about.

Slipping a piece of paper from his pocket, Longarm played his next card by saying, "I've already got a line on a couple of men who are supposed to be good sailors and not too curious, if you know what I mean." He glanced at the paper, which had nothing on it except some scrawled figures that Longarm planned to put on his expense sheet when he got back to Denver. Red Mike couldn't see that, however. "Their names are Carswell and Tarrant. You know 'em?"

"Aye," Mike said, sounding surprised. "At least I did. Who told you about those two, if you don't mind my askin'?"

"A fella up in Galveston, before I came down here. Don't recall his name. Is it important?"

Red Mike shook his head. "No, but you'll not be hirin' Carswell and Tarrant. They're both dead."

"Dead?" Longarm exclaimed. "Son of a bitch. When did that happen?"

"Recently. They were murdered."

Longarm let out a low whistle. "You don't say. What happened?"

"The Kronks got 'em," Red Mike said in a low voice. He seemed somewhat nervous, which was a mite incongruous in such a big, powerful man.

"Kronks?" repeated Longarm, letting his voice rise a little. Several men were looking at him now. He was willing to continue playing the role of stranger in town if it would get the owner and the patrons of the Black Dog to open up to him.

"Cannibal Indians," Red Mike said in an ominous voice. "We thought they were all gone, but they've come back."

"If that's the case, I don't know if I want to do business around here or not."

"Oh, the Kronks won't bother the likes of you, Mr. Parker," Red Mike said hurriedly. "I figure Carswell and Tarrant must've stumbled on 'em by accident. You'll be safe enough here in Rockport."

"I hope so," grunted Longarm. "How did those two sailors die?"

One of the men standing near him at the bar spoke up. "I can tell you that," he said as he thumped an empty beer mug down on the hardwood. "I was with the posse Sheriff Packer took up the other side of Copano to bring back Carswell's body. Tarrant was the same way. Clubbed 'em to death, those savages did, then cut their hearts out and cooked 'em and ate 'em."

"We don't know that part for sure, Albie," Red Mike pointed out.

"Well, what else would they'a done with them hearts?" snorted Albie. "Played catch with 'em?"

Longarm steered the conversation away from that grisly image by asking the man called Albie, "Did you know those boys before they got themselves killed?"

Albie nodded. "Shipped out with both of 'em several times. Not lately, though." The sailor scratched his lantern jaw. "Come to think of it, I hadn't seen either one of 'em for about six months before they turned up dead. Don't know what ships they had berths on, either."

A man on the other side of Albie leaned forward and joined the discussion by saying, "Aye, seemed like Carswell and Tarrant might've dropped off the face of the earth. None of us ever gave it much thought, though, until they turned up dead."

"Well, that's mighty strange," Longarm said. Red Mike was looking at him intently, and he didn't want to push his luck by appearing overly interested in the two dead sailors, so he changed the subject. "I still need a crew, though. What say I come back in here tomorrow night and see who I can round up?"

Red Mike nodded. "Like I said, I'll put the word out."

"Thanks for the drink," Longarm said as he turned away from the bar and started toward the door.

He had only taken a couple of steps when one of the sailors sitting at a nearby table playing poker flung down his cards and exclaimed angrily, "I saw that, ye barnacle-ridden bastard! Ye're dealin' off the bottom!"

"The hell you say!" shot back the man across the table, a rangy cowhand with his wide-brimmed Stetson pushed to the back of his head. "I don't take that kind of talk from anybody, mister!"

"Ye'll take it from me and like it, you cow-lovin'—"

The cowboy's hand dipped toward the gun holstered on his hip as the other players at the table went diving away to hunt a hidey-hole. A few feet away, Longarm stiffened. This wasn't his fight, but any gunplay in this crowded room could have innocent victims—including him.

Before the cowboy could reach his gun, however, the sailor grasped the edge of the table and heaved up with all his strength, toppling the table and shoving it right into the startled cowhand, who fell backwards with a crash. As the sailor started to dart around the table toward the fallen cowboy, another man in range clothes leaped into the fracas, clouting the sailor on the side of the head. The sailor stumbled forward and sprawled on his face as the cowhand who had knocked him down stood above him grinning.

The next instant, another seaman leaped onto the back of the second cowboy, staggering him. The second sailor let out an angry yell and started pounding the cowboy.

It was like a boulder rolling downhill, Longarm thought. Once it got started, there was no stopping it. In a matter of seconds, there was a full-fledged brawl going on in the tavern.

And he was right in the middle of it.

87

Chapter 9

The path to the door was suddenly choked with struggling figures. Red Mike's booming voice roared out, "Stop it! Stop it, you damned fools!" No one paid any attention to him, though. The patrons of the Black Dog were too busy doing some yelling and cussing of their own, along with plenty of punching, kicking, and biting. At least no gunshots had rung out—yet.

Longarm fought to stay on his feet as men crashed into him. He saw a fist whipping toward his head and ducked under the blow, instinct sending his own fist jabbing toward the man who had thrown the punch. Longarm's blow cracked into the man's jaw and sent him staggering backward. He disappeared in the mass of brawlers.

Somebody grabbed Longarm's shoulder and jerked him around. Out of the corner of his eye, Longarm caught a glimpse of the waitresses hurrying behind the bar. The bald-headed bartender was no longer in sight, and Longarm supposed he had done the smart thing and already ducked down behind the hardwood.

That was all Longarm had time to see, because the man who had caught hold of him was swinging a whiskey bottle at his head. Longarm flung up his left arm to block the blow and drove his right into the midsection of his attacker. The man doubled over and backed off, clutching his belly.

Longarm swung toward the door again, but before he could make any headway, someone tackled him. He felt arms wrap around his waist, and then he was going down. He tried to twist free, not wanting to wind up on the floor where he might get stomped and have some real damage done to him. But his shoulder slammed into the sawdust-littered planks and the fella who had tackled him started pelting him with fists like knobby rocks. Longarm fended off the punches as best he could, and managed to send a hard right fist of his own into his attacker's solar plexus. That gave him the chance to arch his back and throw off his opponent like a bucking bull.

He rolled over, pulled himself onto hands and knees, then surged to his feet. Ducking under another punch, he lunged into the man who had thrown it and shouldered him aside. Longarm had gotten turned around, and he saw that he was now facing the bar. He started stumbling toward it, grabbing the collar of a sailor and flinging the man to one side to clear a path. A thrown bottle sailed past Longarm's head and crashed into a mirror behind the bar, shattering it. The room was utter chaos behind him, the air filled with shouts and screams and curses and the sound of furniture being overturned and splintered.

Longarm reached the bar and slapped his palms down on it, steadying himself against the ebb and flow of struggling men all around him. He thought about vaulting over the counter and joining the bartender and the waitresses who had sought shelter back there. Then he considered drawing his Colt and emptying the cylinder into the ceiling. A few gunshots might get the attention of the brawlers and settle things down.

But this wasn't his fight, and all he wanted was to get out of the Black Dog so that he could head off Nora Ridgley if she tried to visit the tavern. Someone on the street outside had probably noticed the disturbance by now and summoned Sheriff Packer, and Longarm expected the lawman would be showing up soon with some shotgun-toting deputies. That would put a stop to the fight quick enough.

Suddenly, a pint-sized cowboy went flying through the air over the bar, tossed head over heels by a behemoth of a sailor. The cowhand slammed into the wall under the shelf where the stuffed corpse of the dog was mounted. The wall shuddered, the shelf shook, and Flounder tipped forward, toppling off his perch to crash down on the bar next to Longarm.

With a roar, the gigantic seaman who had just thrown the cowboy over the bar fixed his rage-filled gaze on Longarm and started toward him in a lumbering charge. The sailor wasn't as big as Hortensio Ortiz's henchman Hector, but near enough so as not to make much difference, Longarm judged. And this fella seemed to be every bit as intent on murdering Longarm as Hector had been.

Longarm didn't want to shoot the son of a bitch, because that might set off more gunfire in the tavern. But he wasn't going to just wait there and let the sailor crush him against the bar, either. With a half-turn, Longarm grabbed hold of the stuffed dog and pivoted back toward the charging sailor, grunting with the effort of lifting Flounder. The grotesque thing must've weighed close to a hundred pounds, Longarm guessed. With a shout of his own, he hurled the dog straight at the onrushing sailor.

Man and dog came together with a resounding crash that sent the big sailor sprawling backward. Flounder landed on his chest and knocked the breath out of him. He lay there under the stuffed animal, and turned red in the face as he struggled to draw air back into his lungs.

Longarm grinned and rested his hands on the bar behind him, then pushed himself up so that he was sitting on the hardwood. He swung his legs around, intending to drop behind the bar and work his way along it until he could reach the front end of it and make a dash for the door. As he dropped to the floor behind the bar, however, the broad figure of Red Mike loomed up in front of him. The tavern owner still had the bung starter in his hand.

"Get out of the way!" Longarm yelled, but Red Mike didn't budge.

"You're not goin' anywhere, Long!" snapped the red-bearded man as he lifted the bung starter.

With a shock, Longarm realized that Red Mike had called him by his right name instead of the alias Longarm had given him. Not only that, but the tavernkeeper clearly intended to clout him one with that bung starter. Longarm wasn't going to stand by and let him do that, even if a shot did lead to more gunfire. His hand swept across his body toward the Colt in the cross-draw rig.

But not fast enough. His fingers had just touched the butt of the gun when the bung starter thudded against the side of his skull. The blow staggered Longarm and made his vision go blurry, as if he had just slipped underwater. He tried again to pull the Colt as he vaguely saw Red Mike drawing back the bung starter for another swing.

Longarm never felt that blow. He was already spiraling down into darkness, his grip on reality slipping away from him just as surely as did the butt of his Colt. He thought he heard a snarling sound, and for an instant thought crazily that he felt Flounder nipping at his heels as he plunged into unconsciousness.

For Longarm, the future was now just a big black dog, growling in the dark.

He felt himself rocking and heard faint splashing sounds all around him. When he finally pried his eyelids open, he found himself surrounded by utter darkness.

Well, that was it, Longarm thought. He'd been knocked clear back into his mama's womb.

After a moment his head cleared slightly, and he realized what an insane notion that had been. He moved one hand a little and felt a rough wooden surface underneath him. He was in the hold of a ship, he decided, and that ship was at sea, judging from the sensations he was experiencing and the sounds he heard.

The only other thing he could be sure of was that his head hurt like a son of a bitch.

He clenched his teeth against the moan that tried to well up his throat. He didn't know if he was alone in the hold or not, but if he wasn't, he wanted to keep the fact that he had regained consciousness to himself, at least for the time being.

Somebody else wasn't being that careful. A deep, hoarse groan came from somewhere nearby. In this stygian blackness, it was difficult to pinpoint a specific direction.

Slowly, Longarm moved each of his arms and legs in turn. He wanted to make sure they were all working, and his efforts also told him he wasn't tied up. That didn't come as a surprise. He would have been willing to bet that the hatch leading out of the ship's hold was barred, and he and anybody else unlucky enough to be down here wouldn't be going anywhere anytime soon.

He pushed himself into a sitting position, moving as quietly as possible. That made his head spin merrily and increased the pounding in his skull until it sounded like gangs of Chinese coolies trying to blast their way through the Sierra Nevadas with dynamite on the old Central Pacific line. Longarm shuddered and waited for his brain to settle down.

When it had—after a period of time that was probably only a few minutes but seemed like hours—he began feeling tentatively around him. He heard another groan, and a moment later his fingers touched something that felt like a flap of leather. It was part of a pair of chaps, he realized as he felt the legs underneath the cowboy gear, and the owner was the one who had been groaning. The man let out another moan and rolled toward Longarm.

Still sitting, Longarm scooted backward until his shoulder blades came up against a wall. That would be either the hull of the ship or a bulkhead between compartments, he figured. He didn't want his companion thinking that he'd been looking for something to steal. They were in this trouble together, and

Longarm knew he might need any ally he could get.

Somebody else muttered a curse in the darkness. So there were more than two of them in here after all, Longarm thought. He was rapidly drawing some conclusions he thought were correct.

A quick check of his holster told him his Colt was gone—just as he had thought it would be—and so was the pocket watch with the derringer on the other end of its chain. He bit back a curse. He'd had a faint hope that his captors might have overlooked the little gun, but that would have been too much to expect, he told himself.

He still had some matches in his shirt pocket, though. He fumbled out one of them and got ready to strike it, squeezing his eyes tightly shut so that he wouldn't be blinded when the match head flared to life.

There wasn't any point in trying to hide the fact that he had come to. He had to find out just how bad the situation was.

A flick of his thumbnail lit the match, and he could sense its glare even through his closed eyelids. He gave his eyes a few seconds to adjust as he heard other men cursing in surprise around him. The sudden light must have been painful to them. He opened his own eyes a slit and peered around the hold.

The scene that met his gaze was about what he expected. The musty hold was approximately twenty by thirty feet, and in that space were lying over a dozen men, some of them still unconscious, others beginning to move feebly, and the rest in varying stages of alertness. Several of them were sitting up and shaking their heads, as Longarm had done a few minutes earlier. Nobody looked too pleased at the situation in which they found themselves.

The man whose chaps Longarm had touched lay a few feet away. He pushed himself up on one elbow, squinted toward the light, and muttered, "What the hell . . . ?"

Longarm thought he looked vaguely familiar, and after a moment he realized that he had seen the cowboy in the Black Dog before the fight broke out. He seemed to recall seeing several of the other men there, too. There was a chance that all of the prisoners had come from the waterfront tavern. Several others were wearing range clothes, and the rest of them seemed to be sailors.

The match had burned down nearly to Longarm's fingers. As he felt the heat of the flame, he shook it out and dropped it with a heartfelt "Damn!" Everything he had seen so far just confirmed what he had suspected as soon as his senses returned to him.

He had been shanghaied.

Well, it wasn't the first time, he told himself. He recalled an assignment that had taken him to the Barbary Coast—

No point in rehashing old memories, a part of his brain reminded him. He ought to be thinking about the future— namely, trying to figure a way out of this damned mess.

He thought about Nora Ridgley, and wondered if she had gone to the Black Dog when she got out of her hotel room. He had hoped to be there to keep her out of trouble, but under the circumstances, if she had visited the tavern she would have been on her own.

He couldn't worry about that now. There was the matter of what Red Mike had said to him to consider. The tavern owner had called him by his right name, which meant that Red Mike had never believed his name was Parker or bought the story about him being a stranger and wanting to hire a crew. Red Mike had just been stringing him along, trying to find out how much he knew.

Which wasn't a whole hell of a lot, Longarm thought bitterly. Obviously, he had turned into a burr under somebody's saddle. Red Mike's? Or had the bearded man been working for somebody else who had tipped him off about Longarm's real identity? And just because Red Mike had been playing him for a sucker, did that mean that everything else he had learned in the Black Dog concerning Carswell and Tarrant had been a lie?

It was all too much to puzzle out. Longarm's head was starting to hurt worse from all the deep thinking. Maybe he could untwist the strands of that knot later, when he got out of the dilemma in which he found himself.

If he got out of it. . . .

"Who in blazes're you?"

The question came from the cowboy nearest Longarm, who said, "I could ask you the same thing, friend."

"Name's Powell, Bob Powell."

"I'm Custis Long."

"Oh, hell, I remember you now, Long. You're that federal lawman who was up at the ranch earlier."

Longarm leaned forward, involuntarily peering toward Powell in the darkness even though he couldn't see hide nor hair of the puncher. "You ride for Circle H?"

"That's right. I saw you when Miss Billie and some of the boys brought you to the ranch house, and somebody told me later you were some sort of marshal. We figured in the bunk house you might've come to see if you could find out what happened to those fellas who disappeared from the ranch. Talk was you were after whoever killed those sailors down by the bay, too."

"That's the case that brought me to these parts," Longarm confirmed. "I reckon we know now what happened to the Circle H riders who vanished."

"What?" Powell asked.

"They got themselves shanghaied, just like we did."

Somebody else exclaimed, "Shanghaied? Son of a bitch! They can't get away with this!"

"Seems to me like they've already done it, old son," muttered Longarm. He heard somebody moving across the deck toward him and stiffened.

A second later, however, Powell's voice said from close beside him, "That don't make sense, Marshal. Those boys who disappeared off the ranch weren't in town when they vanished, and there wasn't no bar fight involved. That's how I got knocked out, and I reckon the same thing happened to you."

"That's right," Longarm admitted. "Think about it, though, Powell. Say a fella wakes up in the middle of the night and steps outside to visit the outhouse. Somebody comes up behind him, taps him on the head, and drags him off into the brush, where somebody else picks him up and carries him down to the bay where a boat's waiting. Simple enough, and it explains how those boys came to vanish without disturbing anybody or taking their gear with them."

"Yeah, I guess so," Powell mused. "But that would mean . . . hell, let me think about this . . . that'd mean somebody on the Circle H is working with whoever's doing the shanghaiing!"

"Yep," Longarm said solemnly. "That's the way it looks to me, too."

Powell obviously didn't want to believe that any of his friends could be enough of a low-down skunk to do such a thing, but the theory made sense. Not that figuring it out did them a whole hell of a lot of good, Longarm conceded to himself. But at least the disjointed parts of the puzzle were starting to come together a little. An organized ring was kidnapping men from the coastal bend area and shipping them out to sea as forced labor. Red Mike was part of that ring, and so was somebody on the Circle H. Was that tied in somehow with the two sailors who had turned up dead on the shores of St. Charles Bay? Likely, Longarm decided, but he had the feeling something was still missing. The whole picture still refused to come together in his head.

Anyway, it was time to turn his attention to other things, like getting out of this musty hold and doing something about his status as a prisoner. He lit another match, after warning the other men he was about to do so, then stood up, swaying unsteadily from the motion of the ship and the aftereffects of the blows to his head. He lifted the match as high as he could and studied the hatch set into the ceiling of the hold. It appeared thick and sturdy, and it was beyond reach, at least six feet above Longarm's head. Even if he could get to it, he probably wouldn't be able to budge it.

But that problem was suddenly resolved, because the sound

of somebody unbarring the hatch came to Longarm's ears. With a grating of wood against wood, it was lifted, and more light spilled down into the hold.

Longarm and his fellow prisoners were about to meet their hosts.

Chapter 10

To eyes accustomed to almost pitch blackness, the light streaming down into the ship's hold seemed as bright as the very heart of the sun. The yellow glow came from lanterns, however, in the hands of a couple of sailors who stood beside the now-open hatch. Two more seamen lowered a ladder into the hold, and a harsh voice commanded, "Climb up out o' there, laddies! But don't try anything, because there'll be guns pointin' at ye the whole time."

For a second, Longarm had thought the voice belonged to Red Mike, but then he realized it was someone different issuing the orders. Whoever it might be was obviously cut from the same cloth. The ruthless arrogance in the voice was very similar to what Longarm had heard in Red Mike's words—just before the tavern owner had belted him over the head with that damned bung starter.

"Better do what he says, boys," Longarm advised the others in the hold with him. "We won't know how bad off we are until we get up there on deck and take a look around."

"I'll go first," Powell said as he got to his feet. When he took a step toward the ladder, though, he suddenly staggered and almost fell. Longarm's hand shot out and grasped his arm, steadying him.

"I'll go," Longarm said. He waited until Powell seemed strong enough to stay upright, then stepped forward, grasped one of the rungs of the ladder, and began to climb.

The ascent didn't take long. As Longarm's head reached the level of the hatch, he darted a quick glance around. Just as he had thought, he was on a good-sized sailing ship. The three masts and the sails they supported towered high over his head. The deck was wide and had rails along both sides at the edges. The hatch where Longarm paused was roughly amidships, a bit closer to the bow than the stern. At least two dozen men surrounded the opening, but most of them weren't armed, Longarm noted.

Five or six *were* holding guns, and that was enough. All he could do for the time being was play along with his captors and wait for an opportunity to turn the tables on them.

"Get on out o' there," said one of the men, and Longarm recognized him by his voice as the man who had spoken earlier. He was short and thick-bodied, wearing a blue coat and a black cap pushed to the back of his head. His face was almost as red as a beet, or maybe it just looked that way in contrast to his white hair and bushy brows and mustache. Deep-set eyes glared at Longarm, who still hesitated.

Another voice growled, "I'll drag 'im up, Cap'n," and a man stepped forward from the ring of sailors. Longarm recognized him immediately as the giant he had knocked down with the stuffed dog back in the tavern. The man flexed his hamlike hands in obvious anticipation of grabbing hold of Longarm.

"That's all right, Uriah," the white-haired captain said. "He's comin', and the others will too if they know what's good for 'em."

Longarm pulled himself on through the hatch and stepped out onto the deck. He motioned for the other men in the hold to follow him. They did so, Bob Powell stubbornly making sure that he was the second one up the ladder, since he hadn't managed to be first. When all of the prisoners were on deck and standing in a tight group surrounded by the armed sailors, the captain tucked his hands in the pockets of his blue jacket

99

and faced them from across the open hatch.

"I'm Captain Jedediah Ransom, and you men might as well get used to the facts right now. On the good ship *Lucy Dawn*, my word is law—and all of ye are goin' to be on this ship until I say different."

"You kidnapped us!" Powell burst out angrily. "You can't do this, you low-down—"

One of the sailors stepped forward and slammed a belaying pin across the back of the cowboy's neck. The blow drove Powell to his knees, and he might have pitched forward onto his face if Longarm hadn't grabbed him. "Steady there," Longarm advised Powell in a low voice. "They're holding all the aces right now."

"I'd like to deal 'em aces and eights," Powell muttered with a grimace as he reached up and rubbed one of his shoulders.

Longarm helped Powell get to his feet again as Captain Ransom went on. "Arguin' won't do ye any good. I got papers on all o' you men sayin' that ye've signed on to work on the *Lucy Dawn* for the next six months. Nobody'll question those papers in any of the ports where we put in, so ye might as well get used to bein' part o' this crew. We're bound for South America, headin' 'round the Cape to Chile."

Longarm had to suppress a groan of dismay. The *Lucy Dawn* would probably stop at quite a few ports along the Atlantic coasts of Central and South America before rounding Cape Horn, but unless Longarm managed to escape somewhere pretty close, it could take him months to work his way back to Texas. In that time, the gang responsible for the trouble in the coastal bend could wreak a hell of a lot of havoc.

Ransom continued. "If ye follow orders, ye'll get along just fine. If not . . . well, my first mate here, Uriah, wields a whip just about as well as anybody ye'll ever see. He can flay the skin off a man's back with a dozen strokes. And if that don't make ye see the light—the sea has a mighty big appetite, lads. It can swallow a man whole and never spit him up again."

The members of the group of captives who were seamen didn't look surprised at any of Ransom's threats. They were

100

accustomed to the iron-handed discipline handed down by the captains of these merchant ships. They would probably accept serving on the crew of the *Lucy Dawn*, even though they had been shanghaied aboard.

The cowboys were a different story. Even though they rode for wages on the ranches where they worked, at heart they considered themselves free. And it was true that a man could always draw his time and ride on if he got tired of his job. It wasn't like being stuck on a ship for months at a time, slaving under harsh taskmasters like Captain Ransom and his first mate. Some of the punchers would never fully submit, no matter what Ransom and Uriah did to them.

And some of them would not survive the voyage, either.

But *he* had to, Longarm thought as he drew a deep breath. He had to live so that he could get away and head back to Texas to finish the job he had started. And although he was still uncertain whether the murders of the two sailors were connected to the shanghai ring, he had a personal score to settle with Red Mike and whoever was working with the gang on the Circle H.

Longarm thought suddenly about Billie Haywood and her father and brother. He hoped none of them ran afoul of the gang. They wouldn't be any match for this vicious bunch.

His mind came back to his own problems, and he heard Ransom saying, ". . . already several miles offshore, so if ye've any thoughts of jumpin' overboard and swimmin' home, ye can forget 'em. The sharks'd be glad to see ye, but they'd be the only ones welcomin' ye."

Longarm looked around. The ship seemed to be alone out here on the gulf. The only other lights he saw other than the lanterns were the moon and stars overhead and a few faint, faint glimmers far to starboard. Those would be lights onshore, he thought, but as Ransom had said, it was much too far to swim. For the time being, he was stuck here on the *Lucy Dawn* as effectively as if somebody had snapped leg irons around his ankles and chained them to the anchor.

"Now get back below," Ransom ordered. "Sorry we can't

offer ye any better accommodations." He laughed harshly, and Uriah and the rest of the crew joined in. One by one, prodded by the pistols carried by some of the sailors, the prisoners climbed back down the ladder into the gloomy hold.

"We can't let those bastards get away with this," Powell muttered as the ladder was being pulled up again. The hatch crashed down a second later.

"Don't worry," Longarm said grimly into the sudden darkness. "I reckon sooner or later they'll see what a big mistake they made when they grabbed us, old son."

From the looks of things over the next few days, it was going to be later. The new members of the crew were watched closely, and there were always armed guards standing by in case of trouble. Captain Ransom, as might have been expected, spent most of his time on the *Lucy Dawn*'s bridge, but Uriah circulated among the crew, making sure they performed their tasks satisfactorily. The threat of a huge, knobby fist was enough to make most of the men toe the line.

Longarm had worked on sailing ships before, and he had not forgotten what backbreaking labor it often was. He spent hours raising sails and then lowering them, often in patterns that made no sense to him. Blisters formed quickly on his hands from hauling on the thick lines that controlled the sails; then the blisters broke and bled so that the ropes were stained red in the places he gripped them. He endured the pain stoically.

But every twinge was one more mark against Ransom and Uriah, one more score to settle when all the debts were finally evened up.

Longarm found himself working most of the time with Powell beside him, along with one of the other prisoners, a sailor called Jenkins. Although Longarm and Powell were disbelieving, Jenkins insisted that life here on the *Lucy Dawn* wasn't that bad.

"I've served on worse ships, and that's the God's truth," Jenkins told them as they hauled in a sail. "Uriah's a right brute, but Cap'n Ransom seems halfway decent. He ain't had nobody flogged just for the sport of it, not yet anyway."

"You sayin' that you don't mind bein' shanghaied?" demanded Powell.

Jenkins shrugged. "We'll get paid at the end of the voyage, just like we'd signed on voluntarily. I was lookin' for a berth when I stopped at the Black Dog and got mixed up in that brawl. One way of winding up on a ship's as good as another, I suppose."

Powell just shook his head, obviously thinking that Jenkins must have gotten into some locoweed.

Longarm said, "I've been thinking about that fight in the Black Dog. Did you see it break out, Bob?"

Powell frowned in thought and then said, "There was an argument between some sailor and a cowhand over a poker game, wasn't there?"

Longarm nodded. "Did you get a look at that puncher?"

"Yeah, I was only a couple of tables away when the fracas started."

"Did you recognize him?"

Powell's frown deepened. "Come to think of it, I don't reckon I did. But that ain't unusual. I don't know every cow nurse in the coastal bend."

"He's not on board this ship, though," Longarm pointed out. "And I've been thinking that fight started mighty convenient-like. I was on my way out of there when the ruckus commenced."

"You think the whole thing was planned?" Powell asked.

Longarm shrugged his shoulders, both to indicate his uncertainty and to ease aching muscles. "Could've been. Red Mike could've tipped off those poker players to start something when he saw I was leaving. I know for sure he knew I was a lawman, because he called me by my right name just before he knocked me out with that bung starter."

Powell stared at him. "Are you sayin' that all the rest of us got grabbed and put to work on this ship just so the gang could get you out of their hair?"

"There's an old saying about killing two birds with one stone."

"Maybe so, but if you're right, the rest of us got you to blame for the trouble we're in."

"Well, then, old son, I'll just have to get us all out of this trouble—"

The scrape of boot leather against the deck behind him was all the warning Longarm got. He started to turn and out of the corner of his eye saw Uriah looming there. The massive first mate's fist crashed against Longarm's jaw and drove him against the railing of the ship. For a dizzying instant, Longarm thought he was going to fall over the rail and plunge into the sea, but then he caught himself and shook some of the cobwebs out of his head. Uriah packed one hell of a punch, there was no arguing with that.

"Get back to work, damn your worthless hide!" Uriah brayed. "The next time I catch you lollygaggin', you'll get a lot worse!"

Longarm rubbed his aching jaw, grimaced, then nodded grudgingly and resumed hauling in the sail with Powell and Jenkins. Uriah swaggered on along the deck.

That was one more mark, Longarm thought.

Each night the prisoners were herded back into their crude cell in the hold. Once the ladder had been pulled up, their supper of hardtack and salt pork was lowered to them in buckets, and every other day a few wrinkled-up oranges were included with the meal so that the men could split the fruit and have a couple of orange wedges apiece. That was enough to hold off scurvy, Longarm knew, but overall the fare was pretty unappetizing. So was the smell in the hold, since the buckets they had to use for slop jars weren't emptied on any regular basis.

As Longarm sat in the darkness, leaning against the hull and trying to sleep, he thought about Hortensio Ortiz and the curse of El Pollo. He reckoned that curse had turned out to be even more effective than Ortiz must have thought it would be. . . .

The *Lucy Dawn* had not put into port since leaving the Texas coast, and as Longarm and Powell and Jenkins went about their tasks several days into the voyage, the sailor pointed to a faint dark line on the horizon far to the west and said, "That's Mexico, you know. We've already passed the border."

That knowledge made Longarm feel even worse. He had been hoping to get off the ship somehow while it was still in American waters. That hope was gone now.

"Where do you reckon we'll be puttin' in first?" Powell asked. "You've been on voyages like this one before, haven't you, Jenkins?"

The sailor nodded. "That I have, lads. The first main port city is Tampico, then Vera Cruz is next."

Longarm suppressed a groan. He knew Tampico was around two hundred miles down the Mexican coast from the border, and Vera Cruz was about twice that.

"We may be stopping at some smaller ports along the way, though," Jenkins went on. "There's no way to know without asking Cap'n Ransom, and I don't believe he'd be inclined to think it was any of our business."

"I ain't never been to Mexico," Powell muttered, pushing back the Stetson he had stubbornly hung on to. "Ain't lookin' forward to it now, either."

Neither was Longarm. If Tampico was the first port of call, that meant he would have at least three hundred miles to cover before he got back to Rockport. And that was only if he managed to get away from the *Lucy Dawn* at the first opportunity.

He was brooding about that when something suddenly struck him in the back of the right knee. That leg buckled, and he fell to the deck, landing with a grunt. Uriah stood over him, bristling with anger.

"We don't give you such fancy accommodations and fine food so you can stand around daydreamin', Long!" bellowed the first mate. "I reckon it's time you learned a lesson, you son of a bitch." He drew back his leg to aim a second kick at Longarm's side.

Even as Uriah's booted foot swung toward Longarm, something snapped in the lawman's brain. He twisted on the planks of the deck and reached out to grab Uriah's ankle with both hands. With a roar of rage, he heaved upward, the unexpected move taking Uriah by surprise and spilling the first mate onto his back. He landed on the deck with a huge crash.

Longarm rolled over and came to his hands and knees, then climbed hurriedly to his feet. Other members of the crew had witnessed his defiance and were running toward him, carrying belaying pins with which to beat him into submission. Fists clenched, Longarm swung toward them to meet this new threat.

Before the other sailors could reach him, however, Uriah sat up and shouted, "Stay back, blast you! He's mine!"

Longarm glanced at the first mate, who was pulling himself to his feet. Uriah's face was suffused with blood and contorted by anger and hatred. He closed his hands into fists and moved slowly but ominously toward Longarm.

"I'm goin' to kill you, mate," he rasped. "I'm goin' to beat you to bloody death."

Captain Ransom's voice lashed out from the bridge. "Uriah! What's going on there?"

"This damned cowboy's finally pushed me too far, Cap'n," Uriah called back as he paused in his advance. "I'm goin' to teach him a lesson."

Longarm flicked a glance at Ransom. The captain seemed to know that Uriah intended the lesson to be a fatal one. After a moment, Ransom gave a short, curt nod.

That confirmed what Longarm had suspected all along. The other prisoners might be allowed to live when this voyage was over, probably would be, in fact. But from the moment he had been knocked out in the Black Dog, he had been intended for only one thing—death. Until now they had just been toying with him, getting as much work out of him as they could. But Ransom had obviously decided that he might as well die now as later.

Uriah took another step toward Longarm, and an ugly grin split his face. "Just you and me, Long," he taunted. "You ain't got no damned stuffed dog to help you this time."

Longarm wondered fleetingly if Flounder was back on his perch over the bar in the Black Dog.

Then there was no time to think about anything except survival, because Uriah lunged toward him, swinging one of those malletlike fists with surprising speed.

Longarm managed to duck under the fist and stepped inside to pound a couple of hard, fast blows into Uriah's stomach. It felt about like punching a bulkhead, Longarm discovered, and did just about as much good, too. Uriah's arms swept around him and tried to lock him in a bear hug that could crush the life out of him.

Longarm didn't wait for that to happen. He let his momentum carry him forward and lowered his head to drive it into the middle of Uriah's face. Blood splashed from the first mate's nose as the butting blow crushed and flattened it. He howled in pain and staggered back a step, giving Longarm a little room.

Longarm used it to bring his knee up sharply, aiming at Uriah's groin. Uriah was able to twist aside in time, however, and took Longarm's knee on his thigh. That staggered the first mate a little more but did no real damage. Uriah had hold of his mashed nose with his left hand, but he used his right to rattle a punch into Longarm's ribs. Longarm stumbled to one side, fighting to keep his balance on the slippery deck.

He was vaguely aware that a crowd had formed around them almost instantly. Most of the spectators were members of the *Lucy Dawn*'s crew, and they were raucously cheering on Uriah. Longarm had his own supporters, though. Powell and Jenkins and the rest of the prisoners were shouting encouragement to him. They had all suffered from Uriah's heavy hand, and they wanted to see him paid back for his brutality.

Longarm didn't care about that. He just wanted to stay alive—a possibility that was in pretty serious doubt at the moment, despite the fact that he had gotten in some good licks.

But the days of hard labor and poor food had already taken a toll on the lawman. His stamina had been weakened, and he was already breathing harder than he liked. His arms were heavy, and he had trouble getting them up in time to block the flurry of punches that Uriah flung at his head. He fell for a feint and let a blow get through that smashed into his chest and rocked him back. He stumbled against something and realized he had fetched up against the railing at the edge of the deck. If Uriah pinned him against the rail, he wouldn't have a chance.

As Uriah came after him, Longarm went down and to the side in a desperate dive. As he went past Uriah's left leg, he caught hold of it and pulled as hard as he could, hoping to topple the first mate again. Uriah was able to keep his feet, though, and he used the height advantage to hammer a couple of punches down around Longarm's head and shoulders. Longarm's hands lost their grip, and he slid to the deck.

Uriah lifted a foot, grinning savagely in anticipation of stomping Longarm to death. Longarm's supporters had fallen silent and watched with grim, stricken faces. As he looked up at Uriah, Longarm's head was swimming, and it seemed all he could do to lift his hands in a futile effort to ward off Uriah's crushing boots.

Filled with confidence and bloodlust, Uriah paused like that, poised to smash Longarm's life out of him. That was a mistake, because Longarm wasn't as far gone as he seemed to be. Longarm's leg snapped out and the heel of his boot caught the kneecap of the leg Uriah still had planted on the deck. There was a sharp snapping sound, and Uriah screamed in pain. He started to fold up, and only a frantic reach behind him caught the railing and held him up.

Longarm rolled over and came smoothly to his feet, drawing on the last of his reserves. He had to finish this fight quickly or die, and he knew this was going to be his only chance. While Uriah was off balance and hanging on to the rail, Longarm bored in, smashing overhand punches, right and left, right and left, past Uriah's attempts to parry them, into the first mate's face. The blows rocked Uriah's head back and forth. He was the one pinned against the rail now, and Longarm rode that horse for all it was worth. His own fists were already aching and swollen, but he ignored the pain and kept crashing them into Uriah's face. He brought his knee up again and this time it found its target, sinking into Uriah's groin with a force that brought another thin scream from the massive sailor. Uriah started to sag forward.

For a moment longer, Longarm held him up with the sheer force of the blows he was landing on Uriah's battered features. Then he stepped back and let Uriah fall. The first mate went down into a huddled ball of utterly defeated flesh.

Longarm stood there over his fallen opponent, gulping down air for his starved lungs. He shook his head, trying to clear away the red haze that seemed to have fallen over his eyes. A pulse pounded in his head louder than a thousand claps of thunder. And he hurt—Lord, did he hurt!

But it wasn't over. Even though the crewmen and the prisoners stood around Longarm, staring at him in near disbelief, Captain Ransom was not stunned into silence. His face even redder than usual from rage, he leveled a shaking finger at Longarm and yelled, "Take him down! Take the bastard down!"

After a second's hesitation, several members of the crew leaped to obey the command. They came at Longarm with fists and belaying pins swinging. Other crewmen pulled revolvers and leveled them at Powell and the rest of the prisoners, just to insure that they couldn't go to Longarm's aid. There would be no mutiny on the *Lucy Dawn* today.

Longarm tried valiantly to fight off the men who came at him, but his strength was gone. His muscles refused to obey his brain, and as the vicious blows slammed into him, he was gradually beaten down. He heard a defiant voice—he thought it was Powell's—shout, "Hang on, Long, I'm comin'!"

A second later, there was a gunshot, the sharp crack splitting the sea air.

Longarm didn't know what had happened to the cowboy, and

he was too close to unconsciousness to worry about Powell. All he knew was that he was surrounded by pain, washing over him like the ocean itself. That was probably where he would wind up, his body thrown overboard to sink beneath the waves and provide a meal for the predators waiting there. And the sad thing about it was that those predators probably weren't as bad as the human ones who sailed on top of the sea. . . .

That was Longarm's last thought as the sailors closed around him, hiding him from sight, and the fists and belaying pins continued for a long time to rise and fall, rise and fall.

Chapter 11

It shocked the hell out of Longarm when he discovered he was still alive.

For a long time, he had been adrift in the sea of blackness that had claimed him during the beating from the ship's crew. But gradually, as he floated back toward consciousness, the pain that gripped him grew stronger, and with it the knowledge that he wasn't dead after all. Dead men were beyond pain, or at least Longarm had always thought so. He'd never talked to anybody who had any direct knowledge of the subject.

He was definitely alive, although when he finally opened his eyes, darkness as deep as his previous oblivion was all he saw.

A low moan escaped his bruised, swollen lips. He tried to roll over but couldn't get his muscles to work. All he could do was lie there on a slimy wooden floor and wonder how come he wasn't dead.

"That you, Long? Must be. Who the hell else would it be?"

The harsh whisper came from somewhere nearby. Longarm thought he recognized the voice. His throat worked convulsively for a moment before he was able to croak, "Powell?"

"Yeah, it's me. I didn't know if you were still alive or not. When they dumped us in here, I figured we was both goners."

"Where . . . where are . . ."

"We're in the ship's calaboose. The brig, Cap'n Ransom called it. It's just a little hole down below the cargo holds. Pretty bad, but I reckon it could be worse. We're still alive."

If you could call this living, Longarm thought. The air was close and fetid, as well as oppressively damp. When he was finally able to roll over after a few minutes, he had barely started to move when he bumped into the hull.

Powell reached out from close beside him and grasped his arm, lifting him into a sitting position. "Don't try to stand up," Powell warned. "The ceiling's only about four feet high. You'll bump your head, and I reckon it's been bumped enough lately."

"Yeah," Longarm muttered. "Are you all right?"

"I'll live. They didn't beat the stuffin' out of me like they did you. When I tried to help you, one of 'em ventilated my arm for me. Then a couple of men jumped on me and wrestled me down, held me until they were through poundin' on you. They dragged both of us down here and dumped us in the brig."

"How . . . how long ago . . . ?"

"That was yesterday afternoon, and I reckon it's nearly night again. You've been out cold for more than a day."

Longarm breathed a curse. That was another day lost, another day for the *Lucy Dawn* to put more miles between him and the coastal bend of Texas. At this rate, he'd be doing good to get back to where he needed to be by Christmas.

Still, he was grateful just to be alive, and it puzzled him why he hadn't been killed. All they would have had to do was toss him over the rail, and he'd be filling the stomach of some fish by now.

"What about that bullet wound of yours?" he asked Powell. "Did they doctor it before they tossed us down here?"

"Nope, but that's all right. I tore a couple of strips off my shirt and tied it up. It's just a scratch. I been hurt a lot worse herdin' cows."

"Thanks for trying to give me a hand—even if it wasn't a very smart thing to do."

Powell chuckled. "You're the closest thing I got to a pard on this here boat, Long. I wasn't goin' to stand there and just let 'em pound you into mush. Not that I was able to stop 'em, mind you."

"Well, you tried, and that counts for a lot. I won't forget it when we get off this floating pesthole."

Powell sounded grim as he said, "We won't ever get off. I saw how Uriah looked when they tossed a bucket of water in his face and brought him around. He's goin' to kill you, first chance he gets. Me, too, more'n likely."

Silence settled down over the brig after that depressing announcement. Longarm leaned back and rested his head against the hull. His skull was filled with a monotonous pounding, and pain shot through his body every time he tried to move, even slightly. His stomach was clenched into a tight, sick ball. He was in no shape to try anything, even if he got the chance anytime soon.

Finally, he asked, "Do they feed us down here?"

"Haven't so far," Powell replied. "Maybe they figure to just let us starve to death."

That wasn't a very pleasant prospect, but Longarm knew they wouldn't have to worry about it. They would die of thirst long before starvation could claim them.

As it turned out, neither one happened. After a couple of hours that seemed like years, there was a grating sound above their heads, and light suddenly slammed into their eyes like a fist, as the hatch leading into the brig was opened. Longarm recoiled involuntarily, bumping his head into the wall as he did so and sending even more skyrockets of pain arcing across his brainpan.

"Are ye ready to come out and act civilized, lads?"

Longarm recognized Captain Ransom's voice. He wanted to tell the captain to go to hell, but he was still too blasted tired. Instead he sat there slumped in silence as Powell said stubbornly, "Let us out o' here and we'll show you just how

113

damned civilized we can be, Cap'n. You can take civilized and stick it right up your—"

An ominous click made Powell fall silent. "That'll be enough. Ye've demonstrated how tough ye are, cowboy. Now come on out and behave yerself so's I don't have to waste a bullet on ye."

"What about Long?" Powell asked.

"We'll get him out too. Perhaps he's learned his lesson, even if ye haven't."

"Well, all right," Powell said grudgingly. "You best take care of him, though. He's hurt mighty bad."

"Let us worry about Mister Long."

Longarm was only vaguely aware of the sound of feet on a ladder, then the feel of strong hands grasping him and lifting him. He seemed to float through the air for a long time before he finally settled down on a surface that was just as hard as the brig but more comfortable because it wasn't slimy. His head was lifted, and something wonderfully soft was slipped underneath it. A folded-up shirt, he would have said if he'd had to guess. Somebody held a cup to his mouth and let some water dribble past his lips, and he sucked at the liquid greedily. After that there was some broth, then a piece of bread that tasted moldy but delicious. It wasn't much in the way of sustenance, but it was enough so that Longarm felt a little strength flowing back into his body.

The life he had led had given him an iron-hard constitution, and he had always been a quick healer. A few days' rest and then he would be back on his feet, he found himself thinking. All he had to do was bide his time.

But time was slipping away, and he fell asleep worrying.

Longarm wasn't given much of a chance to recuperate. The next morning, he was forced out of the hold along with the other men who had been shanghaied back in Rockport. He was too unsteady to climb up into the ship's rigging, so he was put to work in the galley, peeling potatoes. Powell had the same job. An armed crewman stood nearby, guarding against the possibility that either man would use the little paring knives as weapons.

That wasn't very likely. For the first couple of days, Longarm was so stiff and sore from the beating he had received that it was all he could do to hobble around painfully. He was light-headed much of the time, too, and he had to force thoughts through his brain like they were mired in molasses. Powell wasn't in much better shape. The cowboy was flushed and feverish, and Longarm figured the bullet wound in Powell's left arm had festered. Unless Powell got some medical attention—which seemed unlikely—the infection would spread and might threaten his life.

By the evening of the second day, Longarm was starting to feel a little better. His head seemed clearer, and although he still hurt like hell, he was getting around easier. He was still a long way from being in top-notch shape, but at this point he was willing to take whatever progress he could and be grateful for it.

Uriah had been watching both him and Powell like a hawk, just waiting for some excuse to kill them. Longarm still had no idea why they hadn't executed him before now; maybe they just wanted to drag out his torment as long as possible, he mused as he leaned against the hull and ate his meager supper that night. Powell was sitting beside him, but the cowboy was too sick and exhausted to eat.

Jenkins came over and settled down cross-legged on Longarm's other side. The prisoners were allowed to have a small candle in the hold now, and its wavering flame gave off a feeble illumination. Jenkins leaned forward and said to Longarm, "Have you heard the news? We're putting in to port tomorrow night."

"We'll be in Tampico that soon?" asked Longarm.

Jenkins shook his head. "No, we're still several days out of Tampico. The ship's stopping at a fishing village called Punta Rojo. I overheard some of the crew talking about it. They're all quite eager to get there, it seems."

"How come?"

"Evidently they go ashore and take their pick of the village's young women. It sounded like a regular debauch, if you ask me."

Longarm frowned. "And the Mexicans let 'em get away with that?"

"The crew members are well armed," Jenkins said with a shrug. "From what I heard, the ship has stopped there often enough so that the villagers are rather terrorized. They're afraid to fight back."

Longarm could believe that. From Uriah on down to the cabin boy, the crew of the *Lucy Dawn* was about as brutal a bunch as he had ever run across. A small, isolated village of Mexican fishermen and their families wouldn't be any match for the ruthless sailors.

"What about us?" he asked. "I reckon we stay locked up down here, don't we?"

"I would imagine so. I can't believe they would let us out."

Beside Longarm, Powell stirred, lifting his head to mumble, "Whassat? What you talkin' 'bout . . . ?"

Longarm patted the cowboy on the shoulder. "Don't worry about it, Bob," he said gently. "Jenkins and me weren't talking about anything important." Even through the fabric of Powell's shirt, Longarm could feel the heated flesh. Fever had Powell in its remorseless grip.

As he thought about what Jenkins had told him, Longarm found his brain working better then he would have expected. If the sailors intended to go ashore in Punta Rojo for a night of carousing, they would probably leave just a skeleton crew on board the *Lucy Dawn* to guard the prisoners and take care of the ship. If he was going to try anything, that would be the time to strike, Longarm decided. It might have been better if he'd had more of an opportunity to recover from his injuries, but beggars couldn't be choosers. And he wasn't much better off now than any beggar he had ever run across.

Tomorrow night, he told himself grimly. Then he began making plans. . . .

• • •

As Jenkins had indicated, the crew was excited about the impending visit to Punta Rojo, and Longarm heard quite a bit of talk about it the next day. He noticed as the day went by that the shoreline was gradually drawing closer. He wasn't sure if the ship had changed course or if the Mexican coast bulged out more in this vicinity. Late in the afternoon he spotted a reddish-looking promontory with waves crashing around the jagged rocks at its base and decided that was where the village had gotten its name. Sure enough, the small cluster of *jacales* called Punta Rojo—Red Point—was just on the other side of the promontory. As the sun set, the *Lucy Dawn* sailed into the tiny harbor and dropped anchor at the rickety dock extending into the water. Several small fishing boats that were dwarfed by the tall-masted merchantman were also tied up there.

The prisoners were herded below and the hatch dropped closed behind them. Longarm was worried about Powell. The cowboy's condition had grown even worse. He had performed his tasks during the day, but he hadn't said a word. His injured arm was swollen twice its normal size, and it hurt him to move it. His eyes were dull and almost lifeless. He wouldn't last much longer, Longarm judged.

Unless they could get off this damned ship and find some sort of help. There might be a *curandero* in Punta Rojo who could do Powell some good.

Longarm could hear the crewmen trooping off the ship, and the normal footsteps that were audible on the deck over the hold faded away almost to nothing. Just as Longarm had thought, the bare minimum of sailors had been left on duty. None of their footsteps sounded heavy enough to be Uriah's, so he decided the first mate had probably gone ashore with the rest of the men. Longarm wondered if Captain Ransom was still on the ship. The captain was a crafty old son of a buck, and Longarm hoped he was nowhere around. It would be a lot easier to fool some green young third mate.

Longarm had considered several different methods for getting out of the hold, but only one seemed to hold much promise. It would take a threat to the whole ship to make whoever was in charge order that the hatch be unbarred and opened. Anything else would be just laughed off.

The prisoners were busy with their supper as Longarm went over to the spot where the candle sat on the floor in its holder. Earlier in the day while he was in the galley, he had managed to dip his handkerchief in some grease and then stuff it back in his pocket. He pulled it out now, and then took off his shirt, dropping the garment next to the candle. He looked around at the others and asked, "Are you boys ready to get out of here?"

They looked up at him in surprise. "What are you talkin' about, Long?" one of them demanded harshly. "Ain't it enough you been in trouble this whole voyage? Now you're tryin' to get the rest of us killed too?"

"Nobody's going to get killed," Longarm said, although he knew he couldn't make that promise and mean it. The whole thing was too uncertain. "It's time we got out of this hellhole. I hope you're all with me."

"I am." Powell's voice was thick and strained as he pushed himself to his feet. The wounded cowboy swayed and put his good hand against the wall to support himself. "Don't know what you're doin', Long, but I'll back your play."

"Thanks, Bob," Longarm said. He hadn't expected such a show of support from Powell, considering how sick the man was, but Powell was obviously drawing on some reserves of strength from somewhere.

"I'm with you too, Long," Jenkins said as he stood up and came over to Longarm. "What are you going to do?"

"Get us out of here." Longarm held his greasy handkerchief in the candle flame, and it blazed up almost immediately, casting a harsh yellow glow over the hold and giving off some acrid smoke. Longarm dropped the flaming cloth on his shirt, and it caught fire as well.

Startled cries came from several of the prisoners. Nothing was more feared on board a ship than fire, Longarm knew, and with good reason. If the flames spread, a vessel like this one could burn to the waterline in nothing flat. Longarm didn't intend for that to happen, but there was always a chance it would.

His effort to free them might result in everyone on board perishing in a hellish inferno.

But not if he could help it. He threw back his head and bellowed at the top of his lungs, "Fire! Fire down below!"

The shirt was crackling merrily now, and one of the men grabbed a slop bucket, intending to try to put it out that way. Longarm got in front of him and grabbed his arm, stopping him. "Start yelling!" he told the other men. "Really raise a ruckus!"

He didn't have to tell them twice. Everyone in the hold began shouting for help. Even from such a small fire, smoke quickly filled the cramped compartment and made several men cough wrackingly. Longarm moved over underneath the hatch and gestured to Jenkins and another man.

"You'll have to give me a boost up when they open the hatch," he told them. "The smoke'll billow out as soon as they do, so they won't be able to see anything for a few seconds. That'll give us our chance."

"This is insane," Jenkins began, then broke into a broad grin. "But I like it. Get ready, Long." He cupped his hands so that Longarm could use them as a stirrup.

The other man followed suit, and no sooner had they prepared themselves than the grating noise of the bar being removed sounded overhead. The hatch was lifted, sucking the smoke out of the hold, and Longarm heard a man on deck yell, "What's going on down there?"

"Now!" Longarm rapped at Jenkins and the other man. He stepped into Jenkins's boost first and felt himself rising. His other foot found the second man's hands, which pushed him even higher. He reached up, searching for the edge of the hatch.

His fingers slapped against rough wood and hung on desperately. Again wishing he'd had more time to build up his strength, he hauled himself upward as Jenkins and the other

119

man pushed from below. Smoke swirled around him, stinging his nose and mouth. When he sensed he had cleared the hatch with the upper half of his body, he threw himself forward and landed heavily on the deck of the ship.

"Watch it!" someone yelled. "One of 'em just climbed out of there!"

Longarm saw vague shapes around him as he rolled over and tried to get to his feet. Somebody grabbed his shoulder and attempted to shove him roughly back through the hatch. Longarm twisted, catching hold of the man's shirt, and turned the sailor's own momentum against him with a hard yank. The crewman stumbled past Longarm and plunged through the open hatch into the hold with a startled yell.

That yell turned into a scream a moment later as he landed among the waiting prisoners.

Longarm didn't waste any time thinking about the fate of the man he had just tossed into the hold. Instead he lashed out at one of the men around him, feeling his fist connect solidly with a jaw. Arms encircled him from behind, pinning him, and another man charged angrily toward him. Longarm lifted his right leg and met the frontal attack by driving his boot heel into the man's groin. At the same time, he brought an elbow back into the stomach of the man who was bear-hugging him. The man's breath was driven out of his lungs by the blow, and it loosened his grip enough for Longarm to jerk free.

Whirling around, Longarm clubbed the sailor with his left hand while groping at the man's waist with his right. His fingers brushed the textured grip of the revolver he had hoped to find tucked into the sailor's waistband. Longarm grabbed hold of the gun and yanked it away.

He heard something cutting through the air behind his head, and ducked underneath a swung blackjack. As Longarm shoved away the man from whom he had taken the gun, footsteps pounded on the deck and a voice yelled, "Stop him! Kill him if you have to!" He recognized Captain Ransom's enraged tones.

Out of the corner of his eye, Longarm saw movement on the dimly lantern-lit deck, and realized more men were climbing out of the hold. The ladder hadn't been lowered, but now that the hatch was open, they were following his example and boosting each other up. In a matter of moments, the odds in this battle were even, perhaps even tilting over to the side of the former prisoners.

Powell scrambled out of the hold, his injured arm making him move awkwardly, and he was followed by Jenkins. Longarm didn't have time to greet them, because he was busy slapping the barrel of his appropriated pistol against the stubborn skull of one of the *Lucy Dawn*'s junior officers. The man finally crumpled, and Longarm pivoted toward Ransom, knowing he would have to deal with the threat from the captain before he could win his freedom.

Ransom had a gun in his hand, and it was already pointed toward Longarm. The lawman tensed, ready to dive to the deck, but before he could move, Powell bumped heavily into him, knocking him aside.

"Look out, Long!" the cowboy shouted.

At the same instant, Ransom fired. The bullet thudded into Powell's chest with an ugly sound and drove him back. Longarm grated, "Hell!" as Powell collapsed. Before Ransom could pull the trigger a second time, the gun in Longarm's hand roared twice. The impact of the slugs spun Ransom around. He swayed for a second as the revolver slipped from his nerveless fingers. Then he folded up and crumpled to the deck.

Longarm whipped around and dropped to a knee beside Powell. The cowboy's face was contorted in pain, and his chest was covered with blood. Longarm said, "Powell! Damn it, Bob, you didn't have to do that."

A great shudder ran through Powell. His eyes opened as the lines of agony were smoothed away from his features. For an instant, his gaze locked with Longarm's, and then he died.

Longarm took a deep breath and grimaced. He knew that Powell had probably been too weak from the infected bullet wound to live, and a man like the Texan wouldn't have wanted to gasp out the last of his life in a sickbed. Still, Longarm hated to think about the way Powell had died here.

He became aware that flames were licking up out of the open hatch. The fire had spread rapidly, and it was beyond control now. The *Lucy Dawn* was doomed. Longarm and his companions had to get off quickly if they were going to escape.

As he stood up, he saw that most of the former prisoners had done just that. The crumpled bodies of the ship's skeleton crew were sprawled around the deck, along with the bodies of several men Longarm recognized from the long captivity in the hold. Jenkins and a few other men were still on board, but most of the rest of the captives had already fled, leaping from the ship's railing to the old dock. Jenkins hurried over to Longarm and caught at his arm. "We've got to get out of here!" the sailor urged.

"I hear you, old son," Longarm said with a grim nod. He let Jenkins tug him toward the dock.

They climbed onto the railing and then jumped out and down, landing on the pier. Jenkins had gotten hold of a knife somewhere, and he began slashing the lines that held the *Lucy Dawn* to the dock. "The tide will carry her out to sea," he told Longarm. "That should keep the fire from spreading to any of the fishing boats. We don't want to deprive the people of this village of their livelihood."

They had a more immediate worry, Longarm realized as he swung around and looked along the dock toward Punta Rojo. Most of the ship's crew had been in the village when the escape and the fighting occurred, and all the commotion had caught their attention. More than a dozen men were running toward the dock now, led by the towering figure of Uriah.

And in the light of the blazing ship, Longarm could see that the first mate didn't look happy. In fact, he looked downright furious, like he wanted to kill somebody. Longarm knew who that somebody was.

Him.

Chapter 12

"Long!" Uriah bellowed as he reached the dock and paused before coming out onto the warped planks. "I should've known you were behind all this trouble. What the hell have you done?"

Longarm, Jenkins, and their handful of companions stood about twenty feet away, near the end of the dock. The *Lucy Dawn* was slowly drifting away as flames engulfed it. Longarm gestured behind him at the blazing ship and called, "It's over, Uriah. You won't be shanghaiing any more poor bastards to work on that floating hellhole."

Uriah stared at the ship, his brutal face working in disbelief. Suddenly, he yelled, "Cap'n Ransom! Where's the cap'n?"

"That's his funeral pyre you're looking at," Longarm told him curtly.

Slowly, Uriah began to advance onto the dock, trailed by the other members of the crew. His hands clenched into fists as he stared at Longarm. "He told the cap'n to keep you alive as long as we could and make your life a living hell," rasped the first mate. "I knew it was a mistake. I knew we should've killed you right off, you son of a bitch."

Longarm didn't know how much more information Uriah would give away—or even if it would matter in the long run—

but he took a shot anyway, asking, "Who told the captain to keep me alive, Uriah?"

The massive sailor gave Longarm an ugly grin. "He said to tell you just before you died, so I reckon this is the time. It was that little banty rooster, Ortiz. El Pollo."

Longarm's eyes widened in surprise. He hadn't figured that Hortensio Ortiz was tied in with the gang operating along the coastal bend. And yet it made sense. Ortiz was obviously a man of power and influence. Now Longarm knew how Ortiz could afford that fancy estate on the outskirts of Rockport.

"The curse of El Pollo, eh?" Longarm grunted. "Think you can make it come true, Uriah?"

Uriah didn't bother answering the question. He had closed to within ten feet of Longarm. Still grinning, he said, "I'm goin' to enjoy killin' you."

To tell the truth, things didn't look any too good, Longarm thought. He and Jenkins and the others were cornered on this dock, as well as outnumbered by Uriah and the surviving crewmen. The only way out was to jump into the harbor, and then the sailors would just take potshots at them until they had picked off all of the former prisoners. This hadn't worked out quite as well as Longarm had hoped.

Uriah growled and took another step forward.

That was when a rock came flying out of the darkness and cracked into the head of one of the other crewmen. The man let out a yelp of pain, staggered under the blow, and stumbled right off the edge of the dock. More rocks began to pelt the tight knot of sailors from the *Lucy Dawn*. Angry shouts came from the shoreline as shadowy figures darted forward to throw the stones.

Longarm's hopes bucked up like a sunfishing bronc. The people of Punta Rojo, the villagers who had been terrorized and assaulted by the visiting sailors for a long time, were finally fighting back. The sight of the ship going up in flames and floating out to sea must have inspired them. As most of the sailors turned away from the end of the dock to face this new threat, knives joined the rocks being flung through the air. A couple of crewmen clutched futilely at the handles of blades that had suddenly sunk into their chests. Guns began to roar as the sailors struck back at their attackers.

Uriah never turned his attention from Longarm, even as all hell broke loose behind him. The burly first mate leaped forward, swinging a malletlike fist at Longarm's head. Longarm ducked under the blow and cracked the pistol in his hand against Uriah's jaw. The burning ship still gave off enough light for Longarm to see that the bruises on Uriah's face weren't all healed yet. The first mate still bore the marks of the beating Longarm had given him.

But Longarm was still in poor shape himself, and as Uriah crashed into him, he couldn't stay on his feet. Both men went down, landing heavily on the dock and rolling toward the edge.

Longarm got his free hand on Uriah's throat and held on for dear life. With the other hand he slashed the gun at Uriah's head, but the big sailor managed to grab Longarm's wrist and held off the blow. His fingers closed with crushing force. Longarm felt bones grate together in his wrist, and his lips drew back from his teeth as agony shot up his arm.

Neither man knew they had reached the edge of the dock until they were falling. The warm, salty water of the harbor suddenly closed over them as they struck the surface with a great splash. Longarm maintained his grip on Uriah's throat and twisted around until he was on top—at least he *thought* he was. There was no way to know for certain until he arched his back and thrust his head up. His face broke the surface of the shallow water and he gratefully gulped down some air.

Uriah was thrashing and writhing underneath him. Longarm hung on with a strength born of desperation. He kicked at Uriah, but the water robbed the blows of any real impact. Despite that, Longarm knew the water was his strongest ally— as long as he could keep Uriah under it.

Longarm shrugged off the steadily weakening punches that Uriah threw at him. He dropped the gun, since after being submerged it was probably useless now anyway, and tore his right hand loose from the sailor's grip. It joined his left hand around Uriah's throat. Longarm squeezed harder, planted his knees in Uriah's stomach, and held on. Large bubbles rose up, broke on the troubled surface of the water.

Then it was over. A flurry of bubbles abruptly shot up as Uriah's arms dropped back into the water and his body went limp. Longarm was afraid the first mate might be playing possum, so he held on for another minute, gradually loosening his hold on Uriah's neck. More bubbles burst on the surface as water rushed in to replace the last of the air in the big man's lungs.

Longarm let go of the corpse and shoved himself up and away. All of his attention had been focused on the battle with Uriah, and he saw now that he was about eight feet from the dock. The fighting there was over. A mob of villagers in simple homespun trousers and shirts had rushed onto the dock and overrun the sailors from the *Lucy Dawn*. The crewmen who hadn't been knifed had been beaten to death with clubs and rocks. Happy shouts filled the night as the citizens of Punta Rojo celebrated their liberation from the periodic enslavement by the evil men from the sea.

Jenkins was among them, and he turned to the edge of the dock and extended a hand when he saw Longarm slogging back from where he had left Uriah. "Long?" Jenkins called. "Are you all right? You look like a drowned rat!"

Longarm took his hand and gratefully accepted the assistance in climbing back up onto the dock. "Reckon I'll live," he said. He was utterly exhausted, and he felt like he could stretch out right there on those wet planks and sleep for a week.

"Thank God these people finally decided to rise up against those devils," Jenkins said fervently. "I suppose when they saw that the ship was on fire, it gave them the strength to fight back at last."

Longarm nodded grimly and looked toward the *Lucy Dawn*, which had drifted about a hundred yards offshore. The fire had died down considerably now and would soon be out, and what was left of the ship would sink to the bottom of the little harbor.

"Didn't really mean for that to happen," he muttered.

Jenkins leaned closer. "What was that? I couldn't hear you over the noise of the celebration."

The whole village was in an uproar, all right. Longarm heard shouts of laughter and raucous singing. Somebody was playing a guitar, and women were dancing in the street. Punta Rojo was probably a happier place tonight than it had been in a long time.

But that still left Longarm with a problem. He glanced at the burning ship again and wondered just how in the hell he was going to get back to Texas.

As it turned out, that wasn't much of a problem. The grateful people of Punta Rojo put on quite a fandango for their visitors. During the partying, Longarm spoke to the village's *alcalde,* and the mayor immediately suggested a solution. A boat had brought the big man called Brazo Largo to Punta Rojo; a boat would carry him back to Texas where he wished to go. In this case, one of the fishing boats tied up at the village's dock. As soon as the mayor voiced the idea, the owners of the boats began squabbling among themselves to decide who would be allowed the honor of transporting Longarm.

Finally, a wiry young man named Victorio Sanchez won the argument, and early the next morning, while most of the villagers—and the freed prisoners from the *Lucy Dawn*—were still asleep, Sanchez's boat set sail from Punta Rojo, heading north and carrying two passengers, Longarm and Jenkins. The other survivors of the battle were going to stay in the village for the time being.

The young Circle H puncher, Bob Powell, would be staying permanently, along with the other dead men on the sunken ship. Longarm wished he could have recovered Powell's body and given the cowboy a decent burial, but it was not to be. Powell's death was one more mark against Hortensio Ortiz.

Longarm intended to pay El Pollo a visit as soon as he got back to Rockport. And when he did, the feathers were going to fly. . . .

It took six days for Victorio Sanchez's small fishing vessel to reach the vicinity of Rockport and Fulton, hugging the Texas coastline along the way since Sanchez had never been there and had to rely on Jenkins for directions. During that time, Longarm fished from the stern with Jenkins and dozed in the sun, regaining the strength that had been lost during the ordeal on the *Lucy Dawn*. When the boat finally rounded the breakwater and sailed along the beach to the harbor at Rockport, Longarm felt almost like his old self again. He was wearing his own pants and boots, along with a new shirt the grateful villagers had given him, and had a sash of bright cloth tied around his waist. Behind the sash was tucked an old .36-caliber Spiller and Burr Navy revolver he had claimed from one of the bodies of the crewmen killed in the fighting with the Mexicans. He had been away from Rockport for nearly two weeks and hadn't shaved in that time, so he supposed with that much beard and the getup he was wearing, he must look like some sort of pirate.

As Sanchez brought the boat in beside one of the docks, Longarm jumped off lithely and then turned to lift a hand in farewell. "*Muchas gracias,* Victorio," he called to the boat's owner, who grinned broadly and returned the wave. Jenkins said his farewells too, then jumped to the dock beside Longarm.

"Well, Custis, what are you going to do now?" Jenkins asked as they watched Sanchez sail away, the boat steadily dwindling from view.

"I got to go see a man about a chicken," Longarm replied, his jaw tightening. "First, though, I reckon I better drop in on Sheriff Packer. This is his bailiwick, after all."

Jenkins extended a hand. "I'll bid you farewell, then. I can't say it's always been pleasant knowing you, but it's certainly been an exciting experience."

"So long, old son," Longarm said warmly as he shook the sailor's hand. Things might have worked out even worse if

Jenkins hadn't been around to lend a hand with his nautical knowledge.

Longarm was aware some folks were staring at him as he hurried through the streets of Rockport toward Tim Packer's office. The sheriff was probably going to be mighty surprised to see him. The way Longarm had vanished, Packer must have figured that he would never see the big deputy marshal again. Packer could have assumed that Longarm was at the bottom of the ocean somewhere.

Sure enough, when Longarm pulled open the door of the sheriff's office and strode inside, Packer glanced up from his desk, looked down, then jerked his head up again a second later, his eyes wide. "Jehosaphat!" Packer exclaimed. "You ain't a ghost, are you?"

"Nope, I'm real enough," Longarm assured the local lawman with a grin. "I've just been doing some traveling. Went down to Mexico and back, only it wasn't my idea. I was shanghaied."

"Shanghaied!" Packer repeated. "You better sit down, Long, and tell me the whole story."

Longarm did just that, pausing only while Packer got him a cup of strong black coffee from the pot staying warm on the stove in the corner of the office. When Longarm was finished with the yarn, Packer let out a low whistle and said, "I've had a suspicion there was somethin' wrong at the Black Dog for a long time, just ain't been able to prove nothin'. So Red Mike and Ortiz are partners in this bunch shanghaiin' men from the tavern?"

"That's what Uriah told me. Makes me that much more anxious to pay a visit to the little son of a bitch. I figure Red Mike can wait, but if I'm around town for very long, some of Ortiz's boys are liable to spot me and warn him that I'm back."

"Good thinkin'," Packer said with a nod as he scraped back his chair and stood up. "I'll round up some of my deputies, and we'll go see the feller right now. You wait here, where nobody'll notice you."

That idea sounded good to Longarm, so he drank some more coffee and sat in Packer's office while the sheriff went out to find some help for the raid on Ortiz's house. It was early afternoon, the best time for such an action, Longarm thought. Ortiz and his men were probably taking their daily siesta right about now.

If that was the case, they were in for a mighty abrupt awakening.

Packer returned to the office a few minutes later with three hard-faced men following him. The deputies went to a gun cabinet against the wall and began taking down shotguns. Packer said to them, "You boys remember Marshal Long," and the men all gave Longarm curt nods. Packer went behind the desk and opened a drawer to take out a box of shotgun shells. He paused, then picked up a piece of paper and held it out toward Longarm. "Pert near forgot about this. When you turned up missin', I wired your boss up in Denver. Asked him about that Miss Ridgley, too, since she disappeared 'bout the same time you did."

Longarm's head jerked up in surprise. "Nora Ridgley's gone?"

"Dropped off the face of the earth, just like you did."

Longarm cursed under his breath. He had a pretty good idea what had happened. Nora had showed up at the Black Dog after the fight in which he had been knocked out. The amateurish questions she had surely asked had tipped off Red Mike that she was meddling in the gang's affairs. That had probably signed Nora's death warrant, right then and there.

One *more* score to settle, Longarm thought.

Then he took the telegraph flimsy Packer was holding out to him and scanned the words. The message was from Billy Vail and stated tersely that he would send another deputy to look into Marshal Long's disappearance as soon as possible, but Packer should not expect anybody for at least two weeks, due to a temporary shortage of personnel.

As for Nora Ridgley, that was the most surprising part of the wire. Longarm frowned as he read:

BIA DENIES SENDING AGENT STOP ONLY
RIDGLEY AT BUREAU NAMED CHARLES STOP
PLEASE ADVISE MORE INFORMATION STOP

So Nora Ridgley *wasn't* a BIA agent? Then who in blazes
was she? Longarm asked himself.

Maybe El Pollo could shed some light on that.

One of the deputies held out a shotgun, and Longarm took
the weapon, breaking it to make sure both barrels were loaded.
He snapped it shut when he saw the twin cartridges resting in
the barrels.

"Ready?" Sheriff Packer asked grimly, hefting a scattergun
of his own.

Longarm nodded. "Let's go raid us a chicken house."

Chapter 13

As they walked toward Ortiz's house, Longarm wearing a broad-brimmed hat borrowed from Packer, he told the sheriff his suspicions about what had happened to Nora Ridgley. Packer nodded and said, "I reckon you're probably right. For a while I wondered if she'd gone crazy and run off like all them other girls who've turned up missin' lately."

Longarm looked sharply at Packer. "There have been other girls who have disappeared?"

The sheriff nodded and said, "Yep. Remember those folks who were in my office that day when you came to talk to me? They were tellin' me how their little girl had run off, although neither one of 'em wanted to admit that."

"I remember," Longarm said. "There have been others?"

"A whole handful. Not just from around here, mind you, but from Sinton and Taft and San Patricio and some other places too. I been gettin' wires from lawmen up and down the coast and fifty miles or more inland. Folks've settled down a mite from that Kronk scare, but now they're gettin' up in arms about these young women disappearin'." Packer sighed. "Bein' a lawman's gettin' to where it ain't a very pleasant job . . . not that it ever was."

Longarm nodded. Few people carried a badge for the fun of

it, and those that did were probably in the wrong line of work. But somebody had to clean up the world's messes and try to keep things halfway civilized. He and Packer and all the men like them did their best.

An ugly possibility had suggested itself to Longarm as Packer told him about the missing women, but he kept it to himself for the time being. More speculating could wait until after the confrontation with Ortiz.

A few minutes later they reached Ortiz's estate, and as Packer paused in front of the wrought-iron gate in the adobe wall, he motioned to his deputies and ordered, "Thad, you take the back. Thurl and Jimmy, I want one of you on each side of the place. Grab anybody who tries to get away in your direction."

The deputies nodded their understanding and trotted off to take up the positions Packer had assigned them. Longarm said to the sheriff, "I reckon you and me'll go in the front?"

"That's right. You feel up to a little climbin'?"

"I'd rather do that than announce we're here," Longarm said. "I'd just as soon take Ortiz by surprise."

Packer nodded in agreement and handed Longarm his shotgun. "I'll go first," he said.

The sheriff began climbing the gate. His lean, angular figure reminded Longarm of a grasshopper as Packer hauled himself up and over the wrought-iron barrier. Once Packer was back on the ground inside the gate, Longarm passed both shotguns through the bars to him, then clambered over the gate himself.

They went to the heavy wooden door that led into the house. Gingerly, Packer tried the latch and found it unlocked. The door swung open with a faint squeal of hinges; it was next to impossible to keep things from rusting in this damp, salty air. Longarm hoped the slight noise wouldn't be enough to alert Ortiz and his henchmen.

The two lawmen moved into the house, which was much dimmer and cooler than the afternoon outside. The place was quiet, and Longarm wondered if everybody was asleep. A moment later some sort of chanting drifted to his ears. The sound came from somewhere deeper in the house, and with it came a pungent odor. Smoke of some kind, Longarm judged, but it didn't have the clean smell of woodsmoke. Might be incense, he thought.

He and Packer exchanged a glance and then moved down the hall to the big room where Ortiz had greeted them on their previous visit. No one was there, but the chanting was a little louder. Longarm and Packer held their shotguns ready as they started along another corridor.

This hallway led to the courtyard that Longarm had suspected was in the center of the estate. The door at the end was open, and the chanting and the smell both grew stronger as they approached. The lawmen split up, each taking a side of the corridor and hugging the wall as they came up to the open door.

The courtyard was paved with large, flat stones. It was circular, with a narrow flower bed running around the outside of it. In the center was a fountain with a low wall around it and a small statue in the center. Ortiz was on the far side of the fountain. He wore a brown wool robe that must have been hot in the sunshine filling the courtyard. He stood next to a small fire that had been built on one of the paving stones. An iron pot was suspended over the fire. Ortiz had a dead chicken in one hand. The bird still had its feathers on, but its body had been slashed open and Ortiz was solemnly pawing around in its guts with his free hand, from time to time pulling out some grisly dripping bit of the innards and flinging it into the pot. Each time he did that, he intoned something in a lingo Longarm had never heard before, and the chant was echoed by the four young men standing on the other side of the iron pot. Kneeling at Ortiz's feet was a young woman who was stark naked. Longarm's jaw tightened angrily as he recognized her.

Blanca.

So Ortiz had managed to get his hands on the young seamstress after all. Longarm had worried about that during his lengthy absence from Rockport. He should have killed

134

Ortiz when he had the chance, he thought. He had known then that the little man was bad medicine.

Packer was staring wide-eyed at the pagan ceremony Ortiz was conducting, obviously surprised to find that such a thing could be happening in his jurisdiction. Longarm saw the sheriff's knobby fingers clench tightly on the shotgun. Packer didn't like what he was seeing any more than Longarm did.

Longarm wondered where Hector was. The big man wouldn't be very far from Ortiz. But Longarm didn't want to postpone this confrontation any longer, so he would just have to keep an eye out for Hector.

With a nod to Packer, Longarm stepped out into the courtyard. Packer moved to flank him. Leveling the shotgun at the group on the other side of the fountain, Longarm called, "Put down the chicken, Ortiz! You and me got some business to attend to!"

Ortiz stiffened, and his four sycophants started forward angrily, only to stop in their tracks when Packer trained his shotgun on them.

Longarm strode forward and said, "You can get up now, Blanca."

There was no response from the young woman.

Longarm moved around the fountain so that he could see her face. She was staring straight ahead, her eyes dull and listless, her face completely lacking in animation. Longarm grimaced as he realized she had been drugged.

"How dare you intrude like this?" demanded Ortiz. He was so furious that his voice shook and he was trembling all over.

Longarm ignored the question and asked one of his own. "I'll bet you're mighty surprised to see me, ain't you, Ortiz? You figured that I'd be dead by now, either that or still being tormented by Captain Ransom and Uriah."

"I know nothing of these matters," Ortiz said stiffly.

"The hell you don't. Uriah told me that he and the captain took their orders from you. You've been running the ring that shanghais men from the Black Dog and supplies them to ship captains who don't care where they get their crews. You grabbed punchers off the Circle H, too, and sold them into slavery on board those merchantmen. And unless I miss my guess, your gang's expanded lately. Now you're kidnapping young women and doing God knows what with them. Probably selling 'em to whorehouses south of the border."

As soon as the words were out of Longarm's mouth, he knew he had made a mistake by not explaining his theory about the missing women to Sheriff Packer earlier. The sheriff's head jerked around toward him, and Packer exclaimed, "What the hell are you talkin' about, Long?"

With Packer's attention no longer focused on the other four men, they seized the opportunity. Two of them leaped toward Packer, while another one charged Longarm. The fourth and final young man threw himself in front of Ortiz as a human shield. Ortiz finally dropped the dead chicken as he threw back his head and shouted, "Hector!" A string of angry Spanish followed.

Longarm bit back a curse of his own. All hell was going to break loose now, and that wasn't what he wanted. He and Packer couldn't just blaze away with their shotguns, not with Blanca here in the courtyard where some stray buckshot could cut her down. Moving quickly, Longarm reversed the weapon and met the charge of Ortiz's follower. The young man was swinging wildly, and Longarm was able to step inside his attack and slam the butt of the shotgun against his jaw. The man went down like a stone.

Around the fountain, Packer was grappling with the two men who were trying to wrest the shotgun away from him. He cracked a fist full of bony knuckles into the face of one man, knocking him backward, but the other one was able to jerk the shotgun free. The man twisted the weapon, trying to bring it to bear on Packer. The barrels swung toward the sheriff, who reached desperately for his handgun.

Out of the corner of his eye, Longarm saw Packer's dilemma and knew the local badge wasn't going to be able to get his gun out in time. Without thinking, Longarm pivoted at the waist and his free hand swept the Spiller and Burr revolver from behind the sash. The old Confederate handgun bucked against his palm as he fired from the hip. The .36-caliber slug broke the upper right arm of the man with the shotgun, then deflected on into his body and ripped through his lungs. He spun around and tumbled to the paving stones, coughing out his life's blood.

Before Longarm could find another target, he heard the slap of bare feet on the stones behind him, and an instant later something huge and heavy slammed into his back. He was driven forward, his shins striking painfully against the low wall around the fountain. His balance gone, Longarm pitched across the wall and into the water.

Damn it, not again! He was tired of having to fight his battles soaking wet. He tried to get up, but a mountain suddenly moved between him and the sun and fell on him. It wasn't really a mountain, he realized.

It was Hector.

The giant's weight pinned Longarm down and trapped him underneath the water. Longarm remembered how Uriah had died. The situation had been reversed then, and Longarm had been on top. This time, it was going to be *his* air in those fatal bubbles breaking on the surface.

He writhed in Hector's grip, but the big Mexican was just too blasted strong and massive. Longarm was lying facedown, his features pressed painfully against the bottom of the fountain. He had lost the shotgun somewhere when Hector plowed into him, but the revolver was still gripped tightly in his right hand. He worked that arm free from under him and twisted it around so that he could jam the barrel of the Spiller and Burr into Hector's side. It was probably too wet to fire, but he had to take that chance.

Sure enough, the hammer fell harmlessly. Longarm recocked the gun and tried again. With his head underwater, he couldn't hear the soggy clicks the revolver was making, but he knew the weapon wasn't firing. He released it and let it sink in the fountain, then reached behind his head with that hand and tried to claw at Hector's face.

Longarm's chest felt as if it were about to explode. A red mist swam before his eyes. He knew he couldn't last much longer. . . .

Suddenly, Hector seemed to go limp on top of him. That wasn't an immediate improvement, because the big man's deadweight still held Longarm under the water. But then the crushing force went away, and it was like the weight of the world lifting from Longarm's shoulders. He pushed himself up, aware that Hector was no longer lying on top of him. His head broke the water and he took a deep, ragged breath. He shook his head to get some strands of wet hair out of his eyes.

Sheriff Packer and a couple of his deputies stood next to Hector's body, which was sprawled on the stones next to the fountain. There was a bruised, bleeding lump already rising on the back of the giant's head, and Longarm wondered how many times Packer had had to clout Hector with the butt of his shotgun before Hector had passed out. The deputies had climbed over the wall and come running when the commotion broke out, Longarm figured, and he was glad they had disregarded Packer's orders to wait.

Not that the fracas was over. Far from it, in fact, because Ortiz had jerked Blanca to her feet during the confusion and now had the razor-sharp blade of a dagger pressed to the soft flesh of her throat. The one follower he had left who wasn't either unconscious or dead was also still shielding him.

"You will leave this place, Sheriff," Ortiz grated at Packer, "or the girl will die! You cannot interfere with the will of the spirits."

Longarm stepped out of the pool and scooped up the shotgun he had dropped when Hector hit him. "Give it up, Ortiz," he warned harshly. "You're not getting out of here, and you know it."

"I know nothing except that you are a meddling fool!" Ortiz hissed. "I call down the curse of the spirits on you—"

Longarm cut in. "You can take that curse and put it where the sun don't shine, you slick little son of a bitch. You put a curse on me before, remember? You even got your boys Ransom and Uriah to make it come true. But I'm still here, ain't I?" Longarm spat contemptuously. "Face it, Ortiz—when it comes to magic powers, you're flat out of luck."

The self-proclaimed *brujo*'s swarthy face twisted in a grimace of hate. "The blade of this knife has all the magic I need, gringo. It can take this slut's life with one flick of my wrist. And it will, unless all of you leave now!"

"Take it easy, Ortiz," Packer said. "We don't want no more trouble, and if you've got any sense, you don't either. We know you're mixed up with that bunch down at the Black Dog, but if you kill that girl, you'll be a murderer. You'll swing for sure."

Ortiz shook his head. "I spit on your law, Sheriff," he snarled. "I answer to a different power. Raul! Kill them with your bare hands!"

The young man glanced nervously over his shoulder. He looked like he wanted to cut and run, and Ortiz's command to attack the lawmen only made it worse. But Ortiz repeated the order, this time in Spanish, and his tone allowed no argument. If Raul was really a true believer, he had no choice but to obey.

"Don't be a damned fool, son," Longarm said quietly.

Raul swallowed hard, looked at Ortiz again. Ortiz's face might as well have been carved from stone. With a shudder, Raul launched into a run straight at Packer. He howled at the top of his lungs as he attacked.

"Hold your fire!" Packer rapped to his deputies. He stepped aside lithely and let Raul plunge past him. With a quick movement, Packer slapped the barrels of his shotgun into the back of the young man's neck, knocking him forward and down. One of the deputies pounced on him and jerked his hands behind his back, snapping a pair of handcuffs on him.

Longarm saw that action out of the corner of his eye. Most of his attention was still centered on Ortiz and Blanca. The young woman still looked plenty befuddled. She might have been able to get out of Ortiz's grasp—she was bigger than he was, after all—if she had had her wits about her. But whatever drug the *brujo* had fed her had plunged her into a near stupor.

"You're on your own now, Ortiz," Longarm said as he slowly moved forward. "Let the girl go, and we'll talk about the gang operating out of the Black Dog. Were they the ones that killed Carswell and Tarrant too?" The wheels of Longarm's brain were turning over rapidly as he put the theory together on the spur of the moment. "Nobody had seen those two for quite a while, and nobody knew what ship they'd been on. They were shanghaied too, weren't they? Either that, or they were part of the gang and got nervous about what they were doing. Doesn't really matter. Either way, they knew too much and were threatening to talk about it, so you had them killed. You told your men to make it look like the Karankawas had done it so that folks would be scared off from St. Charles Bay. That must be where you move things in and out. Shanghaied crewmen and kidnapped young women went out one way, goods smuggled in from Mexico and South America came in the other. I reckon most of it makes sense now. I knew you didn't get rich enough to afford a place like this casting spells and reading palms and all that other witch-man hokum."

"You lie!" exclaimed Ortiz. "I am a powerful man—"

"You're a dirty little crook, and that's all you are," Longarm said scornfully.

Longarm kept talking for two reasons. He wanted to work out the theory aloud, and he also wanted to give Blanca a little more time to throw off the effects of the drug. He thought he saw something creeping back into her eyes—awareness, perhaps, or maybe just fear as she began to realize that Ortiz was holding a knife to her throat. She was quivering and trembling like a deer caught in the light of a bull's-eye lantern held by a hunter.

Ortiz launched into a string of profanity as Longarm goaded

him. Longarm was just waiting for the right moment to make a move, and that moment came as Blanca's eyes suddenly widened. A couple of seconds ticked by as the danger she was in sunk in on her drug-fogged brain. Then she lifted her hands and grabbed Ortiz's arm. He cursed again and tried to drive the blade into her throat, but she was able to hold it off. She twisted her head and ducked down to sink her teeth into his forearm.

Ortiz screamed in pain as Blanca locked her teeth in his flesh. Longarm sprang forward toward them. With a wrenching motion, Ortiz tore his arm loose. Blood welled from the wound. He shoved Blanca away roughly and turned to meet Longarm's charge.

With a swiping thrust of the knife, Ortiz made Longarm jerk back. The *brujo* tried to seize the momentary advantage and lunged after Longarm. His feet tangled in the long brown robe he wore, though, and he abruptly pitched forward, losing his balance.

Longarm couldn't get out of his way in time. Ortiz fell heavily against the barrels of the shotgun, and the weapon discharged as Ortiz's midsection jolted against it. There was a muffled roar and a thin scream as the twin loads of buckshot blew a hole through Ortiz's middle and obliterated his stomach. Ortiz was thrown back by the blast, and for an instant Longarm thought he could see all the way through the gaping wound in Ortiz's body. Then it was filled with a flood of crimson as Ortiz fell. He landed on his back, arms and legs splayed on the paving stones.

"Well, *shit!*" Longarm said fervently. He hadn't intended for Ortiz to die like that.

Then Blanca's nude, shivering form was in his arms and he was dropping the empty shotgun to fold her into his embrace and hold her while she cried and cried. He stroked her hair and murmured that everything was going to be all right. Packer and his deputies stood around looking half-stunned as they stared at Ortiz and the other dead men. When Packer finally found his voice, he asked, "Do all of your jobs wind up like this, Long?"

"Too damn many of 'em," muttered Longarm. "Too damn many of 'em."

And the worst part about it was, this one wasn't over yet. Not by a long shot.

Chapter 14

One of the deputies gallantly lent Blanca his shirt, although all three of the men looked a little disappointed when she pulled the garment on and covered up all that smooth honey-brown flesh. Then Packer volunteered to take the young woman to his house so that his wife could look after her.

"Not until we've found out a little more about what happened here," Longarm said. Gently, he put an arm around Blanca's shoulders as they both sat on the low wall around the fountain. They were turned so that Blanca didn't have to see any of the bodies, although the smell of burned gunpowder still lingered in the air, blended with the foul odor of whatever that heathen mess in the cookpot was.

Longarm hated to put Blanca through this, but he wanted to know what had happened to her. When he asked her about it, she said hesitantly, "I . . . I came home from measuring Mrs. Hendricks for a dress, and . . . and Hector was there. I tried to scream, but he . . . he put his hand over my mouth. He held me so hard that he hurt me. I thought I would die."

"When was this?" Longarm asked.

"I . . . I do not know. Wednesday evening, I think." Her voice grew a little stronger. "Yes, I am sure. It was Wednesday."

"This is Saturday," Packer said grimly.

"Madre de Dios," breathed Blanca. "I have been been El Pollo's prisoner for almost three days?"

"Looks like it," Longarm said. "I reckon Hector brought you here?"

She took a deep breath and nodded. "Ortiz tried to pretend I was his guest. He had dinner for me, and wine. He forced me to eat and drink. . . . After that, I know little. I remember . . . I remember him chanting and I remember chickens. . . ." She shuddered again. "I think he must have performed many ceremonies. I . . . I may have taken part in them. I do not know."

Packer said, "Well, if you did, it wasn't by your own choice. There ain't goin' to be no trouble about that."

Blanca looked at Longarm and asked, "Do I remember you saying that Ortiz was some kind of . . . of criminal?"

Longarm nodded. "He was part of a gang that was carrying on all sorts of illegal activities around here. I don't know for sure who else was in it yet, but I reckon there was more than one ringleader."

"I . . . I remember something else." Blanca frowned in concentration. "It is just so hard to think. . . ."

"Ortiz drugged either the food or the wine or both," Longarm told her. "Just take your time. Things'll start to come back to you."

"But this is important," Blanca exclaimed in frustration. "I know it is." Her head lifted suddenly, and she stared at Longarm. "I heard cries in the night," she said excitedly. "Cries that sounded like women. And Ortiz said something . . . something about . . . doves? Doves in a cage?"

"Soiled doves," Longarm guessed, feeling his own excitement growing. "The gang Ortiz was in had branched out into white slavery. Could be they've been keeping those kidnapped women right here in Ortiz's house until they were ready to sneak them over to the bay and ship them out." He patted Blanca's shoulder and stood up. "We'd better take a look around," he told Packer.

The sheriff nodded. "Thad, you take Miss Blanca over to my house and tell my missus what happened. Ask her if she'll look after Miss Blanca until I get there. I reckon I'd better stay with the marshal until we get this all sorted out."

The deputy nodded and took Blanca's arm to lead her out of the courtyard. Longarm, Packer, and the other two deputies got busy searching the house. Longarm knew it would be a stroke of unexpected luck if they found the captive women still there, but given what Blanca had said, it was worth a try.

Unfortunately, it didn't pan out. The lawmen searched high and low, all three floors of the sprawling adobe structure, and didn't turn up anything. Longarm found some stairs leading down to a basement, and lit a lamp to take a look down there. Packer followed close on his heels. Once they reached the bottom of the narrow staircase, Longarm shined the light around and saw several thick beams set into the ground. The wood of the beams bore marks where something had scraped against them.

"Chains, I reckon," Longarm grunted, enraged by the idea of innocent young women being imprisoned down here in this dank, gloomy basement. "I'd be willing to bet this is where he kept 'em."

"Well, he won't be kidnappin' anybody else," Packer said. "After seein' this and hearin' what that girl had to say, I can't say as I'm sorry Ortiz got his guts blowed apart. Hangin' might've been too good for the sorry little son of a bitch."

"You won't get any argument from me, Sheriff. Let's get out of here." Longarm started up the stairs and added over his shoulder, "There's no telling how long the women have been gone, but they were here during the past three days or Blanca wouldn't have heard them crying. Maybe we can still catch up to them, or at least find out what happened to them."

"How are we goin' to do that?"

"Time to pay a visit to the Black Dog," Longarm said as he climbed out of the makeshift prison.

• • •

The tavern wasn't doing much business at this time of day. It was too early for the serious drinkers to arrive. But Red Mike was there, alone behind the bar with the stuffed dog back in its place on the wall. He made a grab for something behind the bar as Longarm slapped the door open and stalked into the tavern. As the few customers in the place sprinted for the back door, Longarm leveled the reloaded shotgun at the big red-bearded man and gritted, "You just go right ahead there, Mike. I'm in the mood to blow a hole clear through somebody else."

Red Mike froze, his hand still below the bar. He peered unblinkingly at Longarm for a moment, then swallowed and found his voice. "Somebody else?" he said.

"Ortiz is dead," Longarm said flatly. "You could damn near drive a wagon through where his belly used to be. You can get the same treatment as far as I'm concerned. You had me shanghaied, you son of a bitch."

Slowly, Red Mike lifted his hand from behind the bar. It was empty. He placed it on the bar with his other hand and leaned heavily on them. He said, "It wasn't my idea, Long. None of it was. I just do what I'm told."

"That won't save you from the gallows," Longarm told him grimly.

"Wait a minute, just wait a damned minute! What do you want to know, mate?"

Longarm lowered the shotgun barrels, but only slightly. "That's better," he said. "First off, you knew I was a marshal when I came in here that night, didn't you?"

"Yeah. Ortiz told me. He told me you'd been pokin' around in things that didn't concern you, and that if you showed up in here I was to get rid of you the best way I knew how."

"And that was having me shanghaied along with the other men you roped in during that phony brawl."

Red Mike shrugged his broad shoulders. "I figured we might as well make a little profit and get rid of you at the same time. Sorry, Long. It wasn't anything personal."

146

"The hell it wasn't," Longarm said. "It felt mighty personal when that ape Uriah tried to beat the hell out of me and threw me in a hole on that ship."

"What happened to Uriah and Cap'n Ransom?" asked Red Mike.

"I reckon you know the answer to that. They're dead."

Red Mike nodded. "Figured as much." He sighed. "All right, Long, you might as well get it over with. Go ahead and arrest me. I reckon you got the goods on me. I had those men shanghaied."

The confession came a little too easy, Longarm thought. Red Mike must have been prepared for the law to catch up to him sooner or later, and he was ready to take his punishment for his part in the shanghai ring. That would net him a few years in prison but keep him off the gallows. But there was more to this case than that, and Longarm wasn't ready to close the books on it just yet.

"What about murder?" he asked harshly.

Red Mike blinked at him in surprise. "I didn't kill nobody."

"Those two sailors, Carswell and Tarrant, are dead."

"Yeah, but I didn't have anything to do with that!" Red Mike sounded more nervous now. "I let the gang use my place to snatch those poor bastards who wound up bein' shanghaied, but that's not the same as murder!"

"The gang had Carswell and Tarrant killed," Longarm declared, "and you're the only ringleader left since Ortiz is dead. I reckon you'll hang all right, Mike."

The tavern owner shook his head emphatically. "I tell you, I didn't have anything to do with killin' anybody! I didn't plan anything. I'm not a ringleader! I just took some payoffs and did a few chores. Ortiz gave all the orders!"

"He was the boss of the whole outfit?" Longarm asked sharply.

Red Mike blinked again and frowned. "I . . . I don't know," he finally said after a moment's hesitation. "I sometimes got the feeling that he was just passin' on orders for somebody else. But I couldn't tell you that for sure, Long."

147

Longarm did some frowning and thinking of his own. He had known ever since Uriah had revealed that Ortiz was part of the gang that the little dandy might be the leader, but somehow that possibility had never rung true to Longarm. Ortiz had been arrogant and cruel, and he'd possessed some animal cunning. But Longarm didn't think he'd been smart enough to set up the organization that was operating along the coast.

The identity of the gang's real boss was still unknown, but Longarm was confident now that it *wasn't* Hortensio Ortiz.

"What about Carswell and Tarrant?" Longarm repeated. "Were they part of the gang, or were they shanghaied?"

"They . . . they were part of the gang, I think. They must have tried some sort of double-cross, and that got 'em killed."

"Or they wanted out and were threatening to go to the law," Longarm suggested. "I can see why an hombre might've changed his mind about being mixed up in things once the gang started kidnapping those girls and selling them south of the border."

"Yeah, I can too," Red Mike said, confirming another part of Longarm's theory. "I never liked that part of it either."

Longarm let a faint smile touch his mouth under the beard and the longhorn mustache. "Thanks for letting me know that's what was really going on, Mike," he said. "How many bunches of girls were smuggled out?"

Red Mike stared at him for a few seconds, then spat out a heartfelt curse. "You're a tricky bastard, aren't you? How about if I just don't tell you anything else?"

Longarm lifted the shotgun again. "How about if I just touch off both these barrels? I still need somebody to blame everything on, and I reckon you'll do as good as any."

The tavern owner believed the threat. He licked lips that had suddenly gone dry and said, "Hold on, mate, I'll tell you what I know, I swear. Two shipments of women went south. Ortiz had contacts in Vera Cruz who handled that part of it. Some of 'em wound up in whorehouses in Mexico City, and the rest were shipped on to South America. I don't know what became of 'em there."

Neither did Longarm, and it wasn't something he wanted to think about too much, either. He couldn't do anything for the young women who had already fallen into the clutches of the gang, but he could make sure it never happened again. He said, "The bunch that just went out was only the second one, eh?"

Red Mike looked puzzled and shook his head. "I didn't hear anything about any women being smuggled out lately. The last shipment was nearly a month ago."

Longarm's frown deepened. If Red Mike was telling the truth—and there was no reason for him to lie about it, not after everything else he had already said—then that changed everything. There was a possibility the women Blanca had heard crying while they were being held prisoner in the basement of Ortiz's house were still in the area somewhere. The shipment could be scheduled to go out this very night, in fact.

There was one more question Longarm wanted answered. "What about Nora Ridgley? What happened to her?"

Red Mike stared at the big lawman. He sounded genuinely confused as he asked, "Who?"

"Nora Ridgley. Young, skinny, not too good looking. She claimed to be working for the BIA, and she was planning to come here the same night I got shanghaied."

Red Mike shook his head. "Sorry, mate, I got no idea what you're talkin' about. I didn't see no woman who looked like that in here the night we grabbed you, nor any night since."

Again, there was no real reason for him to be lying. Longarm's jaw tightened. If Nora hadn't disappeared because she was snooping around the Black Dog, then what had happened to her? And who was she, really, since it was obvious from Billy Vail's telegram that she wasn't working for the Bureau of Indian Affairs, as she had claimed?

Damn it, Longarm thought. Every time he thought he had this case just about unraveled, the strands got all twisted up again.

But he had done all he could here at the Black Dog, so he stepped aside from the doorway and said, "Come on in,

Sheriff. I reckon you heard enough to lock up Red Mike here for a long time."

Tim Packer stepped into the dim interior of the tavern and said, "I damn sure have. Step out from behind that bar, Mike, and come along with me."

"Sure, sure," muttered Red Mike. Keeping his hands in plain sight, he moved along the bar and emerged from behind it. As he walked past Longarm and Packer, both of whom kept him covered with their shotguns, he said again, "I swear I didn't know anything about the killin's, and kidnappin' all those girls wasn't my idea."

"You'll have your day in court," Packer told him. "Now move along."

Red Mike was the first to step out into the late-afternoon sunlight, followed by Packer and then Longarm. As Longarm emerged from the tavern, he heard a faint, faraway bang. Ahead of him, Red Mike's head snapped back and the burly tavern owner grunted. He stumbled forward a couple of steps, and then pitched forward to land on his left side in the crushed shell of the road.

Before Red Mike's body hit the ground, Longarm had grabbed Packer's shirt collar and jerked him backward. The lawmen sprawled back through the door of the tavern as Longarm said urgently, "Stay down, Sheriff!"

Packer already had the same idea. Both men rolled away from the open door and came to rest on their stomachs, shotguns lifted and ready to fire. Not that they were going to be able to put up much of a fight with scatterguns. The shot Longarm had heard, the shot that had killed Red Mike, had come from a long ways off, far out of shotgun range.

"What the hell happened?" Packer demanded in the silence that had fallen.

"Somebody just made sure that Red Mike wouldn't remember anything else important to tell us," Longarm said bitterly. From where he lay, he could see the huddled shape of the bushwhacked tavern owner. Red Mike's face was turned so that the left half of it was pressed against the crushed

150

shells, but the right half was visible to Longarm. He saw the look of surprise frozen on Red Mike's face for all eternity. And he saw the black-rimmed hole in the man's forehead leaking a worm of crimson that crawled steadily into the ground. Considering the distance involved, it had been a hell of a shot.

After a few minutes, Packer asked, "I reckon that bush-whacker's long gone by this time. What do we do now?"

Longarm stood up slowly and solemnly regarded the body of Red Mike. "Fetch the undertaker, I reckon," he said.

"I meant about this damn mixed-up case of yours," Packer snapped.

Longarm sighed. "I don't know, Sheriff," he said. "I just don't know. . . ."

Chapter 15

Once Longarm thought about it, the brick wall he had seemed to be facing wasn't quite as tall and impassable as he had first taken it to be. While he and Packer were waiting for the undertaker's wagon to arrive, he did some thinking out loud. "There's still those women the gang kidnapped. According to Red Mike, they haven't been sent south yet."

"Not that he knew of," the sheriff pointed out. "Sounded to me like he didn't know everything that was goin' on around here, just the part that had to do with him."

"He knew about the first two bunches," Longarm argued. "I think he would have heard about this last one too if the women had been smuggled out already."

"Maybe so, but what good does that do us?"

Longarm scraped a thumbnail along his beard-stubbled jawline as he thought, then tugged distractedly at an earlobe as his frown of concentration deepened. "Whoever's running this whole shebang knows I'm back from Mexico and not dead after all. He must've found out that we caught up with Ortiz and that Ortiz is dead. Now the boss is covering his tracks as best he can—that's why Red Mike was killed. He was dead as soon as the boss saw us come out of the tavern with him. My thinking is that he'll try to lie low for a while now and hope that everything blows over. He doesn't know for sure what Ortiz and Mike told us before they wound up defunct. Maybe he's hoping we'll blame everything on Ortiz and Red Mike and he'll be off the hook."

"Yeah," Packer said with a slow nod as he struggled to follow Longarm's line of reasoning. "How's that put us any closer to him?"

"Like I said, he's still got that bunch of kidnapped women on his hands. Until they're safely at sea and on their way south of the border, he's got to worry that somebody will find out about them. That's the one weak link still in the chain," Longarm said emphatically.

Packer looked skeptical. "You're basin' a lot on the hope that them women are still around here someplace," he said dubiously.

"When a hope's the only one you've got, it starts to look a hell of a lot better than it might otherwise." Longarm grinned. "I'm going to leave you to tidy up here, Sheriff, while I do a little scouting around. First, though, I need some firepower besides this Greener."

"There's Winchesters and Colts at the office, and plenty of cartridges for all of 'em," Packer said as he dug in his vest pocket and took out a small key. "That'll unlock all the cabinets. Help yourself, Marshal. You sure you don't want me to come along with you?"

"I'll holler for help if I need it. Besides, I want you to keep a close eye on Blanca for me. If the fella behind all this knows she was at Ortiz's place for the past three days, he's liable to come after *her*, too, just on the off chance she might be able to tell us something important. Which she already has, of course, but that's one thing the boss can't know yet."

Packer nodded. "I'll see that no harm comes to her. Where are you headed?"

Longarm gazed toward the northeast and said, "This whole thing seems to have revolved around St. Charles Bay. That's where Carswell and Tarrant were found, and I still think the gang killed them there and made it look like those cannibal

Indians were involved because they wanted people to steer clear of that area. Got to be a good reason for that."

"If I don't hear from you later this evenin', I'm comin' to look for you," Packer said.

Longarm nodded. "Good idea. Because if you don't hear from me, Sheriff, I'm liable to need all the help I can get."

Longarm went by the sheriff's office first and picked out a rifle and a handgun from the cabinets along the wall. Both weapons fired .44-40 cartridges, so he took a single box of ammunition to go with them. With the revolver tucked behind the sash he was using in place of a belt, the Winchester in one hand, and the box of shells in the other, Longarm strode down the street toward the Rockport House.

The same clerk was on duty, and he stared wide-eyed as Longarm stalked across the lobby. "Where's my gear?" the lawman demanded. He didn't figure the hotel had let his room sit empty the past couple of weeks just on the hope that he might come back someday.

"It . . . it's in the storeroom," the clerk stammered. "None of us thought we'd ever see you again, Marshal."

"Well, I'm back," Longarm said, "and I want some clean clothes and a belt instead of this damned sash. I'm tired of looking like I ought to be prancing around a stage and singing songs in some Gilbert and Sullivan operetta. I'm a deputy United States marshal, blast it!"

"Yes, sir, you certainly are," the clerk said hurriedly. "If you'll come with me, I'll take you to your things and you can get whatever you need."

Longarm accompanied the nervous clerk into a storage room underneath the stairs, then used the hotel office to change clothes once he had found what he wanted. When he emerged, he was wearing clean socks, underwear, and trousers, and he had on one of his own shirts instead of the one he had borrowed in Punta Rojo. The Colt was tucked behind a belt that had been loaned to Longarm by the desk clerk. Longarm would have preferred wearing a holster, but he didn't want to take the time to look for one. Besides, the gun rode in a rough approximation of the position it occupied in his normal cross-draw rig. He still wore the hat Packer had loaned him.

Despite the fact that delaying even more chafed at him, Longarm paused long enough to say to the clerk, "I hear that Miss Ridgley disappeared the same day I did. Anything you can tell me about that?"

The clerk shook his head. "I'm afraid not, Marshal." His voice took on a slight chiding tone as he went on. "She left the hotel after our handyman took her door off its hinges so that she could get out of her room. Someone had jammed a key in the lock and broken it off."

Longarm grunted. Obviously the clerk suspected him of that mischief, but there wasn't time now to explain. "She didn't say where she was going?"

"Not at all. She just handed me her key and said that she had an appointment. She was rather angry, I recall. She said she hoped the gentleman didn't think she had forgotten about him."

Longarm growled a curse and suppressed the impulse to grab the clerk and slap the silly look off his face. The smug little son of a bitch had just told Longarm something important after claiming not to know a thing about Nora Ridgley's disappearance. Of course, Longarm reminded himself, the gent might not be smart enough to realize the importance of what he had just said.

Nora had been meeting somebody.

Now that Longarm thought about it, he recalled seeing her in the hotel after the first time they had wrangled, and a man had been with her then, too. They'd had their backs to Longarm, but Nora had definitely been with a man. That hombre had to be tied up in all this somehow. Maybe *he* was the one responsible for her vanishing.

Something tickled at the back of Longarm's brain, then slipped away. His teeth clenched in frustration, but he knew from long experience that there was no way to force these things. He would figure it out when the time was right and not before. Until then, all he could do was forge ahead.

Besides, the problem of Nora Ridgley's disappearance was a cold trail. He had a more promising lead in the kidnapped women.

With a nod of thanks to the clerk, Longarm hurried out of the hotel lobby and turned toward the nearby livery stable. He wanted to rent a horse—on credit, since he didn't have even a peso on him at the moment—and get started north toward the ferry at Copano Bay as soon as possible.

Ten minutes later he was riding out of Rockport on a mouse-colored gelding. The stable owner· had already heard gossip to the effect that Longarm was back in town, and he was willing to provide the horse in return for a promise of payment later. The government was good for the debt, he told Longarm.

Longarm didn't disabuse him of the notion that that was always true; he was just glad to get the horse. He followed the road along the shoreline until he reached the mouth of the bay and the ferry landing. The sun was still at least an hour from setting as he drew rein and called out in the direction of the little shack that served as the ferry company's office, "Hey! Anybody in there?"

The old man who had been on duty at the landing the last time Longarm made the crossing came limping out of the shack and muttered, "Hold your horses, hold your horses. Now what d'you— Say, ain't you that marshal feller?"

"That's right. Where's the ferry?"

"Over at t'other landing. You need to get across the bay?"

Longarm bit back an impatient reply and said, "As soon as I can."

The old man nodded. "I'll run up the flag. That'll let Johnny know to come across. He's my grandson, you know."

"No," Longarm said with a shake of his head, "I didn't." Nor did he care, but he kept that thought to himself.

The old man began pulling on a line that lifted a bright red flag to the top of a short flagpole. He looked over his shoulder at Longarm and asked, "You ever find them Kronks?"

156

"No. I don't think there are any around here. Somebody else killed those two sailors." He wished the garrulous old-timer would get on about his business and stop asking questions. Longarm didn't want to be forced to explain the whole complicated mess.

"Well, I don't know about that. But there's Kronks around here, you can take my word for that. I ain't sure they ever all went away, the way folks said they did."

Longarm's mind wandered as the old man nattered on. The facts of the case seemed to point not only to St. Charles Bay but also to the Circle H ranch, which bordered the bay. He had decided that the gang had an inside man working on Jesse Haywood's spread, since punchers had been disappearing from there, too. That inside man might be the ramrod of the whole outfit, Longarm thought. Whoever it was would have easy access to the bay where the smuggling ships moved in and out—assuming there was any smuggling going on, and Longarm was convinced of that as well. The gang had their fingers in a lot of pies: the white slavery operation and the shanghai ring for sure, and probably the smuggling of illegal goods as well. When everything was added up, it would be a lucrative setup for the man running it.

And the fact that it was an operation fraught with human misery wouldn't mean a damned thing to the cunning mind that had dreamed it all up.

Longarm intended to point that out to the son of a bitch, and right strenuously, too.

The ferry finally arrived, and Longarm led the mouse-colored gelding on board. The crossing seemed interminable, but at last he swung up into the saddle and rode off the steam-powered ferry, heading for the trail that led down to St. Charles Bay.

His route took him past the huge live oak he had noticed the first time he came over here, and he reined in sharply as he approached the big tree this time. There was a black stallion tied to a bush near the tree, and a figure stood underneath the spreading branches. Longarm recognized both the horse and the young woman with long blond hair. She turned to face him and stared at him in surprise.

"Marshal Long?" exclaimed Billie Haywood.

Longarm walked his horse toward her and tugged on the brim of his hat. "Howdy, Miss Haywood. Good to see you again."

She shook her head in confusion. "We had heard you disappeared. Talk around town was that the Kronks had gotten you."

"Not hardly," Longarm said with a grin. "But it's a long story. What are you doing out here, if you don't mind my asking?"

Billie shrugged. "I come here to the big tree sometimes when I've got a lot on my mind. It helps me get my thoughts straight, I guess." She turned toward the tree and gestured at its massively thick trunk. "It's been here for hundreds of years, you know, standing strong through all the hurricanes and everything else time could throw at it. Legend has it this is one of the places where the Karankawas sacrificed their victims and ate their hearts. There must have been a lot of blood to soak into the ground and feed those roots."

Those were mighty gruesome thoughts to be occupying the mind of a pretty young woman, Longarm thought. He said, "I reckon people could find some dark and bloody ground just about any place they went. Humankind's a mighty violent species most of the time. I like to think there's some decency in most folks, though."

Billie regarded him thoughtfully. "I'd think a man in your line of work would be completely cynical about people, Marshal Long. You see so many bad things."

"Call me Longarm. And I see some good things along the trail too, Miss Haywood."

"If I'm going to call you Longarm, you have to call me Billie," she said, and the brooding expression she had been wearing disappeared totally as a smile lit up her face. "I'm glad the Kronks didn't get you after all. What brings you over here, Longarm?"

"I'm looking for somebody." He had to tell her part of it if she was going to understand his mission. "There's an organized gang that's behind the deaths of those two sailors, as well as just about everything else bad that's been going on around here. That fella Ortiz was part of it, and so was Red Mike, the gent who owned that tavern, the Black Dog."

"Was?" Billie repeated.

"They're both dead," Longarm said flatly. "They had a boss, though, and I think he might be whoever's been working with them as an inside man on the Circle H. You see, those punchers who disappeared were snatched and sold as sailors to ship's captains who didn't care where they got their crews, as long as they came cheap. Men got shanghaied from the Black Dog for the same reason." Longarm hesitated, hating to break bad news to her. "There was a fella named Powell . . ."

"Bob Powell," Billie said immediately. "He vanished over a week ago." Her eyes widened. "Are you saying that Bob was . . . what did you call it, shanghaied?"

"I'm afraid so. And I'm afraid he's dead too. He was killed helping me and some other fellas escape from the ship where we were being held prisoner."

Billie's hand went to her mouth in shock. "Bob Powell dead? That's terrible! He . . . he was always friendly to me." Tears rolled down her cheeks as her eyes suddenly filled with moisture. "And you say somebody on the Circle H is responsible?"

"That's what it looks like to me. I hated to have to tell you that, Billie, but—"

"Let's go," she said suddenly as she used the back of her hand to wipe away the tears. She strode over to her horse and jerked the reins loose, then swung up into the saddle. "Let's head for the ranch house and get to the bottom of this. If you're right, somebody's going to pay. Nobody betrays the Circle H."

Longarm was glad she wasn't angry at him. She looked mad enough to spit fire right about now. He fell in alongside her as she rode away from the big tree. They headed across an open pasture north of the live oak, skirting a slough that meandered up from the bay.

They were about halfway across the pasture when somebody started shooting at them from some trees on the other side of the slough. Longarm heard the first shot at the same time as a bullet whined past his head. More slugs thudded into the ground around the feet of their horses. As he hauled the gelding around, Longarm called to Billie, "Come on! Back to that tree!"

The big live oak was just about the best cover they were going to find around here, and they were definitely going to need a place to fort up. Longarm leaned forward as he galloped back across the pasture. He threw a glance over his shoulder and saw Billie riding beside him. Her face was pale with fear, but her jaw was clenched determinedly. The big black was taking the ground in long, efficient strides, and Billie began to pull ahead slightly as more lead searched for them. From the sound of the shots, there were several riflemen hidden in those trees.

Longarm cussed himself as he rode. The boss of the criminal outfit must have had men watching the ferry and the trails leading to the Circle H. That lent even more weight to Longarm's theory that the inside man on the ranch was the brains of the whole operation.

Of course, having that theory confirmed wouldn't do him a damned bit of good if he caught a rifle bullet in the back. He hunched even lower over the gelding's neck as something plucked at the borrowed hat and knocked it right off his head. That bullet had come too damned close. . . .

Billie had almost reached the tree and Longarm was about ten yards behind her. Suddenly, the black stallion screamed and leaped high in the air in mid-stride. One of the bullets had found Billie's mount, Longarm knew. He shouted, "Billie!" as the young woman was flung out of the saddle. Luckily, she had kicked her feet free from the stirrups when the stallion was hit, so she wasn't pulled down with the horse as it collapsed and rolled over. Instead she flew through the air to slam into the ground near the base of the huge live oak. Longarm threw himself from the saddle and was running toward her as soon as his boots hit the ground.

He didn't reach her. Something slammed into the side of his head and sent him tumbling forward into blackness as deep as that in the hold of the *Lucy Dawn* had been. Vaguely, he tasted dirt in his mouth and knew he was lying on the ground beside the big tree.

Dark and bloody ground, he had called it. And as consciousness slipped completely away from him, he knew that once more blood was staining that ground, just as surely as it had in the days of the Karankawas.

His blood . . .

Chapter 16

Longarm didn't know how many more knocks his poor old noggin could take. Good thing his skull was as thick and hard as it was, or his brain would be about the consistency of cold grits by now.

But he was alive and thinking fairly clearly, and he was damned grateful for that. Now if he could just figure out who was wiping his face with a wet cloth. . . .

There was one way to do that. He could open his eyes, he supposed. But that was liable to hurt like hell. The darkness enfolding him was a lot more comforting.

Still, he didn't have any choice, and he knew it. He took a deep breath and forced his eyes open.

The lean features of a gray-haired man were peering down at him anxiously. "Thank the Lord," the man said fervently. "You're alive, Marshal Long. I was afraid you would never wake up."

The man seemed familiar somehow. After a moment, Longarm recognized him, but not before managing to croak out, "Where the hell am I?"

"Not Hell," Father Terence said with a faint smile. "Although under the circumstances some might take it for such."

Indeed, now that he was more alert, Longarm could hear the

sort of weeping and wailing that was usually associated with fire and brimstone. He cast his eyes from side to side, looking past the priest to see thick stone walls and heavy beams on the ceiling of the windowless room where he lay on the floor. "We're in the mission, aren't we?" asked Longarm.

Father Terence nodded. "This is the vestry. Those men threw you in here when they brought you and Miss Haywood to the mission."

"Billie!" Longarm exclaimed. "Is she all right?"

"She's bruised and rather shaken up, of course, but she's not seriously injured," Father Terence assured him. "On the other hand, I thought you were dead when they first brought you in, Marshal. There was blood all over your head. Once I cleaned that off, however, I could see that the bullet had only creased you."

Longarm lifted a hand to his head and felt the strip of cloth wound around it as a bandage. "Thanks for patching me up, Padre," he grunted. "What's going on here? Who's doing all that crying I hear?"

"The women," Father Terence replied, as if that explained everything. When Longarm still looked confused, he added, "The ones who were brought here earlier today, when those gunmen chased away my flock."

Longarm wondered if he would think a little straighter sitting up, so he pushed himself upright despite the priest's warning to be careful. From that position, he could see through the open doorway of the vestry. The sight that met his eyes cleared up some of his confusion. He saw half a dozen women, all of them young and pretty, with their hands and ankles tied. They were sitting against the far wall of an adjoining room, and they all looked scared to death. Worse, they looked like they had been scared to death for a long time.

"The gang brought 'em here from Ortiz's place to wait for the ship that's going to come in tonight to pick them up," Longarm guessed.

"That's what I gather. I'm afraid you know more about all of this than I do, Marshal Long. All I know is that men with

163

guns came earlier today and frightened off the poor people who work here. I refused to leave, however." Father Terence touched his own head lightly, and for the first time Longarm noticed the ugly bruise at the priest's temple. "I'm sure they intend to kill me once they're through here."

"Maybe not," Longarm said. "You might wind up working as a deckhand on some ship bound for South America. This bunch doesn't pass up many chances to turn a profit."

He pushed himself to his feet, with Father Terence grasping one of his arms to steady him. He had been disarmed again, Longarm saw. That was getting damned annoying.

With the priest's help, Longarm made it to the doorway of the vestry. Now he could see that there were over a dozen young women being held prisoner in the other room. Billie was among them, tied hand-and-foot like the others, and when she saw him, she exclaimed, "Longarm! Are you all right?"

"I reckon I will be," he told her, trying not to sound as bleak as he felt.

There were four men with rifles in the room, two of them dressed like sailors, the others looking like typical range-land hardcases. One of the men dressed cow pointed a Winchester at Longarm and said harshly, "Sit down against the wall there, lawman, and don't even think about tryin' nothin'. We got to keep these gals alive, but the boss said we could shoot you if we have to."

"Mighty thoughtful of him, singling me out like that," Longarm said dryly. But he sat down beside the wall as he had been commanded to do. Father Terence sank down cross-legged beside him.

Billie Haywood's wasn't the only familiar face among the captives, Longarm realized as he looked over the young women. To his surprise, Nora Ridgley was there too, tied like the others. He supposed that the whorehouse owners in Mexico and South America could find a use for just about any female, even one as skinny and plain as Nora. Unlike the others, she wasn't crying. She seemed to be asleep, her head tilted back against the wall. But her lips were moving, and Longarm realized after a moment that she was praying, not sleeping.

After a few minutes, Nora opened her eyes and looked across at him. "Hello, Marshal Long," she said.

One of the guards spoke up. "Here now, the boss didn't say nothin' about lettin' you talk to this lawman. Best keep your mouth shut."

"I'll speak to whomever I please," Nora said stubbornly. "I'm not afraid of you."

The man stepped closer to her and lifted the rifle, threatening her with the butt of the weapon. "You damned well better be afraid of us, bitch. If you wasn't so bony, we'd have us a little fun with you 'fore you get shipped off down south."

A voice came sharply from the door that led outside. "Leave her alone," it commanded. "There's no need for that."

Billie Haywood cried, "Frank!"

Her brother strode into the room, followed by four more men. Frank Haywood's hair was disarranged, as it had been the last time Longarm saw him, and his spectacles had slipped down on the bridge of his nose. He had his hands clasped together behind his back as he went over to Nora and asked, "Are you all right? Did anyone hurt you?"

"Not yet," she replied bitterly. "But you can stop pretending, Frank. You don't care. You never cared. You fooled me with your . . . your charm."

Frank Haywood had never struck Longarm as charming— but then Longarm wasn't a woman, either. And he never would have guessed that the inside man on the Circle H was so far inside as to be the owner's son. But Frank's tone of command as he entered the mission had been unmistakable, and it still was as he began issuing orders.

"Get them ready to go," he told his men. "The ship should be arriving in less than an hour."

"Frank!" Billie said desperately. "What . . . is . . . going . . . on . . . here?"

He turned to face his sister. "I'm sorry, Billie, I really am," he said. "You were in the wrong place at the wrong time. But I couldn't take a chance on Marshal Long stopping here at the mission and discovering what I've been doing."

"I already know what you've been doing, Haywood," Longarm said heavily. "You're the boss of this bunch. You've been sitting up there in that tower of yours and pulling everybody's strings. Some young women kidnapped here, some men shanghaied there, a little smuggling on the side . . . it was a damned smooth operation for a while, wasn't it? You could see the comings and goings along the bay, and you knew when it was safe for your ships to sneak in at night. You had it all figured." Longarm laughed humorlessly. "But you were wrong about that big storm you said was coming. It never hit."

Frank's face twisted slightly as he glared at Longarm. "Perhaps it's just not here yet," he snapped.

"Frank," Billie said shakily, "is it true? Is all that Longarm said true?"

"I'm afraid so."

"But *why?*"

His features stiffened into a taut mask. "I never wanted to run the ranch. You know that. So Father was disappointed in me. *You* were more of a son to him than I ever was. Both of you thought my interests in science were ridiculous." He shrugged. "So I made my own mark, made it my own way."

"But this . . . this thing you've been doing . . . it doesn't have anything to do with science."

"Of course not. There's no money to be made in forecasting the weather. And that's how everyone judges success. Power is money, and money is power. It follows as surely as rain follows an area of low barometric pressure."

Well, it was absolutely certain now, Longarm thought. Frank Haywood was crazy, crazy as a loon.

But that didn't make him any less dangerous.

"You know, I saw you with Nora back there in Rockport, when all this started," Longarm said to Frank. "I didn't get a look at your face, but it was you, right enough. And I kept thinking later I had seen something that was the key to the whole thing. I just never could come up with what it was."

"Well, that was lucky for me and unlucky for you, wasn't it?" Frank said with a slight smile.

"He began paying attention to me almost as soon as I arrived in Rockport," Nora said bitterly. "I suppose he heard that I was asking questions about those men who were killed, so he decided to keep tabs on me by playing up to me." There was pain in Nora's eyes as she went on. "I've never been used to a great deal of . . . of male attention. I was so flattered that I couldn't see what he was doing."

"Don't feel too bad, Nora," Frank told her. "I really did enjoy your company. You're an intelligent woman."

So far the other men had not acted to obey Frank's order to get the women ready to move. They were obviously waiting for him to quit talking to the prisoners. Longarm wanted to draw things out as long as possible; night had fallen, as he could see through the open door that led outside, and Sheriff Packer might be on his way over here even now to look for him.

"There's a few things yet I don't understand, Haywood," Longarm said. "Why move these women from Ortiz's place? Wouldn't it have been safer to leave them there, rather than commandeering the mission and letting Father Terence know what you're up to?"

"That was your fault," Frank snapped as he turned back to face Longarm. "One of my men spotted you in Rockport when you were getting off that fishing boat. He sent word to me right away. When I heard that you were back, I figured you might know about Ortiz's part in the organization, so I had the women moved immediately. This old mission was the most convenient place to the bay where they could be hidden. Actually, I was glad that you killed Ortiz; his superstitious nonsense had become quite bothersome, and I was hoping you'd lay the blame for everything on him."

"I thought about it," Longarm admitted. "The whole thing didn't feel right yet, though, and after I'd talked to Red Mike, I knew somebody else was involved. Did you shoot Mike yourself, Haywood?"

Frank nodded. "I have a rifle with a telescopic sight. I'm

167

quite good with it. I've grown accustomed to using a telescope in my weather observations. When I saw you and Sheriff Packer come out of the tavern with Red Mike, I was afraid it might be too late already, but just in case he hadn't revealed anything important yet, I thought it best to remove him from the picture."

Billie was crying tears of disbelief, anger, and fear. Longarm didn't know how close she and her brother had been, but it had to be devastating for her to sit there and listen to Frank so calmly discussing murder and kidnapping and wholesale villainy. It just went to show, Longarm thought, that you could never really know folks without getting inside their brains— and so far, that was pretty much impossible.

Longarm turned his attention to Nora. "While I've got the chance," he said, "I want to know about you, Miss Ridgley. According to the BIA, you don't work for them at all. The only Ridgley in the agency is named Charles."

Frank looked at her sharply. "Is that true, Nora? You told *me* you worked for the Bureau of Indian Affairs too."

"Charles Ridgley is my father," she said stiffly. "He's been in the same low-level position in the agency for years. I thought if I could discover whether or not there were really Karankawas in this part of the country again, Father could take the credit and finally advance his career. I . . . I know he's been terribly frustrated."

So she was nothing but an amateur, Longarm thought, an amateur meddling in the case for purely personal reasons. He swallowed a curse of frustration that tried to come up his throat. As bad as things were now, there was no point in making Nora feel even worse, and cussing her foolhardiness wasn't going to make things any better for the rest of them.

"I kept trying to steer you away from anything important, Nora," Frank was telling her. "But when you insisted on going to the Black Dog, I knew something had to be done about your interference. I was truly sorry . . . and I still am."

"Save your apologies," she told him angrily. "You're nothing like what I thought you were, Frank Haywood. Nothing!"

His slender face hardened, and he nodded abruptly. "If that's the way you want it," he said. He turned to the guards and the men who had come in with him. "I told you to get them ready, blast it!"

"Sure, Boss, sure," one of the men said. He jerked his head toward the others. "Let's go."

One by one the sobbing women were lifted to their feet and the bonds around their ankles were cut. Longarm hoped that at least some of them would make a break for freedom, but no one even tried to reach the door and dash out into the night. They were all too cowed to put up any form of resistance, he saw.

He said to Frank, "You're sending Miss Ridgley south of the border. What about your sister?"

"Billie? I'm sorry about that, too." Frank looked at her. "We've had our differences growing up, but I honestly care about you, Billie. You've got to go with the others, though. There's too much at stake to turn you loose."

"You'd damned well better not turn me loose, Frank Haywood," she shot back at him. "I'd shoot you myself!"

"Oh, I know that quite well. You always chose the straightforward solutions, didn't you, Billie?"

She looked away and didn't answer him. Her chin was trembling with either fear or rage, or maybe both.

Longarm said, "What about me? Am I being shanghaied again?"

"That didn't work the first time," Frank said with a shake of his head. "No, I'm afraid you'll have to die here, Marshal. You and Father Terence will be killed, and your hearts will be cut out. The Karankawa scare has faded somewhat, and it's time to bring it back even stronger than before. No one will ever come near this place again once your bodies are found."

Frank's voice was calm and cold and full of scientific detachment. It was a shame things had gotten all twisted around in the boy's brain and soul, Longarm thought. Frank Haywood might have accomplished some great things in his life—if he hadn't been a crazy killer deep down.

"Take them out," Frank told his men, jerking a thumb at the young women. The captives were herded out at gunpoint, including Nora and Billie. Nora stared straight ahead and refused to look at Frank as she went past him, but Billie glared at her brother and said, "I hope Dad never finds out what a low-down skunk you turned out to be. Go to hell, Frank!"

He just stared stonily at her and motioned for the men to take her on out of the mission. One of the guards stayed behind with his rifle trained on Longarm, much to the big lawman's disappointment. If all the men had left with the prisoners, then Longarm was planning to jump Frank. As it was, Longarm thought, he was going to have to try something anyway. He couldn't just sit there and wait calmly for his own death as those women were led away and sent on a journey that would end only in a living hell for them.

Just as he was about to surge to his feet and make a desperate leap for the man with the rifle, there was a sudden shout outside. A gun went off, followed by a scream of pain. More shots sounded.

Frank jerked around toward the door, and so did the guard. Longarm knew it might be his only chance. He came up off the floor and flung himself at the man with the rifle.

The guard heard him coming and tried to whirl back around, but he had only made it halfway when Longarm crashed into him. Longarm slammed a punch to the man's head as both of them went down. His other hand closed around the barrel of the Winchester and tried to wrest it loose.

Frank Haywood let out a startled cry and started toward the struggling figures, but Father Terence was on his feet and got in front of him. "Get out of the way, Padre!" Frank shouted as he threw a punch at the priest's head.

Father Terence ducked under the blow and tackled Frank, knocking him back. It was obvious the man of God was no fighter, but he was doing the best he could.

That gave Longarm the chance to smash a right and a left into the face of the guard and knock him out cold. Longarm snatched up the rifle and twisted around on his knees just as Frank tore away from Father Terence's awkward grip, smashed the priest in the face with his clubbed fists, and darted toward the door. Longarm snapped off a shot that whipped past Frank's head and slammed into the thick stone wall of the mission.

There was still a lot of yelling and screaming going on outside, although the shooting was sporadic by now. Longarm bounded past Father Terence, who had sunk to his knees, stunned by Frank's blow. As Longarm reached the doorway of the mission, the rifle gripped tightly in his hands, an unexpected sight met his eyes. The Mexican peasants he had seen laboring in the mission's gardens on his first visit, the same peasants who had been chased off earlier in the day by members of Frank Haywood's gang, had returned.

And they had returned with a vengeance.

Using machetes, pitchforks, and hoes, the Mexicans had obviously struck from hiding in the trees around the mission, attacking the gang when the men emerged from the church with the prisoners. The women had broken away and were waiting on the other side of the clearing in which the mission sat, watching wide-eyed as their former captors were stabbed and hacked to death. Several of the Mexicans had been shot, but they outnumbered Frank's men at least two to one and had overrun the gang. Farming implements became deadly weapons, and the blades were daubed with blood as they rose and fell.

Frank Haywood wasn't going to wait around for the same fate to befall him. He leaped to one of the horses tied nearby and vaulted into the saddle as he jerked the reins loose. Leaning forward over the animal's neck, he drove his heels into its flanks and sent it plunging into the night at a frantic gallop. Longarm threw a couple of shots after him, but the sound of the racing hoofbeats never broke stride.

"Damn!" Longarm bit out. The latest victims of the white slavery ring were safe now, but the ringleader was getting away.

All the shooting was over, the men who had been with Frank all dead except the one Longarm had knocked out inside the mission. Still clutching the Winchester, Longarm ran over to Billie and Nora and asked, "Are you two all right?"

Both women had been watching the grim spectacle of the gang members being finished off with horrified fascination. Billie nodded and said, "We're not hurt, Longarm. What are you going to do now?"

"Go after that brother of yours."

Billie shuddered. "He's no brother of mine. Not anymore."

"Can you look after these women?"

"I'll see that they get safely to the ranch. We can take care of them there until we get word to Sheriff Packer about what's happened."

Billie was still shaken by everything she had seen and heard tonight, but Longarm could tell her natural strength was asserting itself. He nodded, squeezed her shoulder, and then turned toward the horses. Frank already had a couple of minutes' lead on him.

But Longarm had seen the awkward way the young man sat a saddle, and he figured Frank wasn't the most experienced rider in the world. Longarm was confident he could catch up, or at least draw within rifle range.

Frank knew the ins and outs of this coastline with all of its bays and coves and marshes, however. He knew the surrounding terrain perhaps better than anyone. There was a chance he could give the lawman the slip unless Longarm caught up with him quickly. Picking out a strong-looking bay that had belonged to one of the dead outlaws, Longarm swung up into the saddle and galloped off into the night in the same direction Frank had gone.

He rode with the Winchester in his right hand and the reins in his left, ducking instinctively as Spanish moss that dripped from low-hanging branches brushed his face. After a few minutes of pushing the bay as fast as he dared over unfamiliar ground in darkness, Longarm reined in and listened intently. The beat of hooves came to his ears from up ahead somewhere.

172

He grinned. He was still on Frank's trail, all right.

As he pushed on, he thought about the evil Frank Haywood had brought to the coastal bend, and that made it easy to ignore the pain throbbing in his head. This case had really put him through the wringer, but he sensed that it was just about over now. One way or another, tonight was the final showdown.

Suddenly, his keen eyes picked out a couple of things ahead of him in the light from the moon and stars that washed down over the landscape. He saw the big tree where he and Billie had been captured—and he saw Frank riding toward it at a breakneck pace. Longarm jerked his mount to a halt and brought the rifle to his shoulder to try a shot.

The Winchester kicked heavily against his shoulder as he pressed the trigger. He couldn't tell if he had hit his target or not, but Frank's horse abruptly swerved. Longarm saw Frank grab frantically at the saddlehorn, but he was unable to stay aboard the now-bucking animal. Longarm knew his slug must have creased the horse and made it crazy with pain. Frank slid off and pitched to the ground, landing hard in the shadows underneath the massive live oak.

Longarm kicked the bay into a run again and headed toward the tree. He saw Frank stagger to his feet, and a second later flame geysered from the barrel of a pistol as Frank fired. Longarm didn't know where the bullet went, but it didn't come close enough for him to hear it. He called out, "Drop the gun, Frank!"

Instead, Frank fired again, and this time Longarm heard the whine of lead cutting through the air near his head. He was within thirty feet of the tree now. He kicked his feet out of the stirrups and threw a leg over the saddle as Frank triggered another shot. The bay galloped on as Longarm dropped from the saddle and landed on his feet. His momentum carried him forward and he let himself go, pitching to the ground as Frank's gun blasted yet again. This bullet passed over Longarm's head, and he knew Frank was finally getting the range.

"Give it up, damn it!"

Frank wasn't listening. Snarling a curse, he lowered his aim at the prone lawman.

Longarm didn't give him time for another shot. He fired the Winchester, levered the rifle, fired again. The .44 slugs smashed into Frank's chest and sent him stumbling backward. He was still trying to bring his pistol to bear on Longarm, even though he was mortally wounded. Longarm jacked another shell into the Winchester's chamber and fired again, and this time the bullet drove Frank all the way back against the wide trunk of the tree. The pistol finally slipped from his fingers, and he followed it to the ground, sliding slowly down the trunk, leaving a dark smear of blood on the tree's bark. He came to a stop in a sitting position, legs splayed out in front of him, his head and shoulders hunched forward.

Longarm got to his feet and approached slowly, ready to fire again if need be. But when he prodded Frank's shoulder with the barrel of the rifle, Frank slumped lifelessly to the side.

Far out over the gulf, thunder rumbled and lightning flickered. Longarm saw it and knew there would be a storm later. Whether or not it was the one Frank had predicted would strike, there was no way of knowing.

Longarm had a feeling the weather where Frank was now was dry and mighty hot. . . .

He rode up to the mission a little later with Frank's body slung over the horse behind his saddle. There was a fire burning in front of the little stone building; Longarm had seen the glow of it several minutes earlier as he approached and wondered what was going on. He wasn't expecting what he found.

There was no sign of Billie, Nora, or the rest of the young women, and Longarm hoped they were safely on their way to the Circle H. Father Terence was standing in the doorway of the mission, however, holding his head in his hands and looking sick. Longarm rode around the fire and the people gathered beside it and came up to the mission.

Father Terence turned his face toward Longarm and said, "I tried to stop them. I swear I did. They're peaceful people, but they were finally pushed so hard they went back to their old ways. We might be dead now if it wasn't for them, but still . . . God have mercy on all of us."

Longarm nodded grimly and looked at the peasants he had taken for Mexicans earlier. He had never gotten a close look at them until this moment, however, and now he could tell they weren't Mexicans at all.

Not all the Karankawas had left the coastal bend. Some of them had probably stayed here at this mission all along, Longarm thought, converting to Father Terence's religion and living a peaceful existence—until they had been forced out of it. The high cheekbones lit by the dancing flames of the fire revealed their heritage.

And so did the hearts of the dead men, which had been hacked out of their bodies and were now skewered on sharp sticks and roasting over those flames as the Kronks capered around in anticipation of their feast. . . .

Longarm shuddered. "God have mercy," he echoed.

Because the Kronks sure as hell hadn't.

Chapter 17

Longarm was in the parlor of the Circle H ranch house again a couple of days later, wearing new store-bought clothes and saying his good-byes to Jesse Haywood and Billie. He extended his hand to the old cattleman and said sincerely, "I'm sure sorry about everything that happened, sir. Wish it could've turned out different."

Haywood nodded. "So do I, Marshal. So do I."

The rancher seemed to have shrunk even more into his wheelchair since Longarm's first meeting with him, and Longarm knew the discovery that his son had been some sort of criminal mastermind had been mighty hard for Haywood to swallow. If Haywood was like most folks, he was probably blaming himself, at least in part, for the way Frank had turned out.

Haywood confirmed that by saying softly, "He was always a strange boy. I never quite knew what to do with him. I . . . I should have done things differently, I reckon."

"My mama always said things turn out the way they do for a reason," Longarm told him. "There's an old song that says farther along we'll know more about it. There's a lot of truth to that."

Haywood nodded. "Yes. I suppose that's right."

Longarm said good-bye to the old man, then walked out of the house with Billie beside him. For the first time since Longarm had known her, she was wearing a dress instead of denim pants and a man's shirt. It was a black mourning dress, but she still looked lovely.

"Are you ever coming back this way, Longarm?" she asked as he went to his horse.

He paused beside the animal and turned to look at Billie. "I hope the trail leads back to these parts sooner or later," he said honestly, "but in my line of work a fella can't ever be sure of that."

She put a hand on his arm. "I'd like to spend some time with you again, when things aren't so . . . so . . ."

He knew what she meant. Gently, he put his hand under her chin, tilted her head back slightly, and kissed her, a soft kiss, warm with the promise of things to come. "I'd like that too," he told her.

But that would be sometime in the future, if ever, and in the meantime he had to get back to Denver. He'd been away longer than he had ever expected to be on this assignment, and even though he had wired Billy Vail with the news that things had been cleared up satisfactorily, Longarm knew his boss would likely have another chore for him once he returned.

He squeezed Billie's shoulder, swung up into the saddle, and rode away from the Circle H with a wave of farewell for the young woman who stood there watching him. A special young woman indeed.

Two nights earlier, Billie had shepherded the group of former captives from the mission to the ranch house, then sent a rider to fetch Sheriff Packer as fast as possible. That Circle H cowboy had run into the sheriff and a pair of deputies just disembarking from the ferry over Copano Bay, and he'd led them back to the ranch at a gallop. By that time, Longarm was there too, with Frank Haywood's body, and the next few hours had been an ordeal of explanations. Longarm knew he would never forget the look of stunned horror on old Jesse Haywood's haggard face as the rancher found out the truth about his son.

All in all, Longarm thought now, the only thing that was really satisfying about this case was that it was over.

He made one more stop on his way back to the ferry. Father Terence greeted him in front of the mission. The fields nearby were empty. Longarm nodded toward them and asked, "Your people run off again?"

"Yes, but I'm sure they'll return once they come to grips with what happened to them. They took their canoes and paddled off into the gulf. I had no right to stop them."

"Nope, I reckon not."

The priest looked at him intently. "You didn't tell the authorities the truth about them, did you?"

Longarm rested his hands on the saddlehorn and leaned forward. "Wouldn't be any point in that, would there? I don't see any Kronks around here now, and I don't know if anybody would believe me if I said they used to be here. No, Padre, your secret's safe with me."

"All these years," Father Terence murmured. "I really thought they had changed. I thought I had gotten through to them."

"Folks can sometimes change what they do," Longarm said. "They can't change who they are."

Father Terence managed to smile slightly. "You sound like a philosopher, Marshal."

Longarm grinned back at him. "Nope, just a lawman." He ticked a finger against the brim of his hat, added, "So long, Padre," and then turned the horse and rode away.

He was back in Rockport in plenty of time to shake hands with Sheriff Packer and bid the local badge-toter farewell, then catch the stagecoach that took him back to Corpus Christi. When he strode into the train station there, he saw a familiar figure waiting on one of the benches.

"Well, howdy, Miss Ridgley," Longarm said to the woman as he came up to her. "I figured you were already on a train headed back East."

"I knew you'd be coming along soon, Marshal, so I decided to wait," Nora Ridgley said with a smile. She seemed to have recovered from the ordeal of her captivity, except for a faint, haunted look in her eyes. She went on. "According to the train schedule I studied, we can travel together for part of the journey."

"Oh?" Longarm slid a cheroot out of his vest pocket, put it in his mouth without lighting it, and sat down beside her, his brand-new war bag at his feet. "That sounds mighty pleasant."

"I was hoping you'd think so." Nora hesitated for a few seconds, then continued. "I'm sorry for all the trouble I caused, Marshal. I was just trying to help my father. I . . . I hope you understand."

"It all worked out in the end," Longarm assured her. "Except you didn't find any Kronks."

Nora sniffed. "Karankawas! I think they were just a figment of everyone's imagination. Thank goodness their day is long since gone."

Longarm just nodded sagely. Nora could think whatever she wanted to.

After a moment, she said, "Marshal . . . if I may be so bold . . . would you like to have dinner with me on the train?"

Longarm grinned around the cheroot. "Ma'am, you can be as bold as you want, and I'd be pleased to have dinner with you. But my friends call me Custis, or Longarm."

"All right. And I'll even forgive you for locking me in my room that night, although it was certainly a naughty trick."

"Yes, ma'am, I allow that it was."

"And call me Nora."

"Yes, ma'am," Longarm said.

So they traveled together part of the way and had dinner together . . . and breakfast . . . and Longarm discovered that

Nora Ridgley could be bold, all right, and that she knew some naughty tricks of her own. She wasn't quite as skinny as he had thought, and those plain features became a lot more attractive once he realized that lurking behind them was about as wantonly erotic an imagination as he had ever run across.

And although there was a lot of man-eating going on, not once did Longarm think about those blamed old cannibal Indians.

Watch for

**LONGARM AND
THE SAN ANGELO SHOWDOWN**

193rd in the bold LONGARM series

Coming in January!

A special offer for people who enjoy reading the best Westerns published today.

WESTERNS!

NO OBLIGATION

Mail the coupon below

To start your subscription and receive 2 FREE WESTERNS, fill out the coupon below and mail it today. We'll send your first shipment which includes 2 FREE BOOKS as soon as we receive it.